THE
MYSTERY TRAIN
DISAPPEARS

KYOTARO
NISHIMURA

THE
MYSTERY
TRAIN
DISAPPEARS

DEMBNER BOOKS • NEW YORK

DEMBNER BOOKS
Published by Red Dembner Enterprises Corp.,
80 Eighth Avenue, New York, N.Y. 10011

Distributed by W. W. Norton & Company, Inc.,
500 Fifth Avenue, New York, N.Y. 10110

Library of Congress Cataloging-in-Publication Data

Nishimura, Kyōtarō, 1930–
    [Misuterī ressha ga kieta.   English]
    The mystery train disappears / by Kyotaro Nishimura.
       p.   cm.
    Translation of: Misuterī ressha ga kieta.
    ISBN 0-942637-30-5
    I. Title.
    PL857.I78M5713   1990
    895.6'35—dc20   90-3302
                                             CIP

Misuteri Ressha Ga Kieta, the original edition of this novel, was
published by Shinchosha, Tokyo.

The Mystery Train Disappears was translated from the original Japanese
edition by Gavin Frew.

Design by Antler & Baldwin, Inc.

CONTENTS

TOKYO STATION

1

Tokyo Station, August 8, 11:30 P.M.

The last train for Ogaki leaves platform nine at eleven twenty-five and after that, the platform generally remains deserted until the following morning. Today, however, was special; the Mystery Train was due to leave at one minute to midnight and the platform was overflowing with people.

The Japanese National Railways, or J.N.R. as they are generally referred to, run at a constant loss and are often likened to a dying monster. Some of the newer services, like the world-famous bullet trains, show large profits, their operating costs accounting for only about sixty percent of their income, but on average, the system's operating costs are equal to one hundred fifty-five percent of the annual income, which means that the more trains they run, the more money they lose.

In an effort to increase their earnings, J.N.R. puts on all kinds of attractions and special trains, the latest of which was today's Mystery Train. Being a Mystery Train, of course, nobody knew what its destination was and the advertising had only given the following information:

Departure: Tokyo Station, Saturday, August 8, 23:59.
Return: Monday, August 10, 09:30.
Utilizing "Blue Train" type-B sleeping cars there will be amusements provided en route. Available seats, four hundred. Adults ¥ 30,000; children half price. All applications to be made by post.

The fact that nobody knew where the train would be going seemed to appeal to the public, and there were over twenty applications for each available seat. There was no age limit, so couples in their twenties as well as old-age pensioners applied. The passengers were chosen by lot and were notified one month before the train was due to leave, the tickets being issued two weeks later.

Kenichi Tsuyama, a reporter for the travel magazine *Ryoso*, climbed the stairs to the platform with one of his colleagues, Yukiko Norikane. He had been ordered to cover the story of the train by the chief editor, Taguchi, but J.N.R. was not issuing any tickets to the press and so he had had to ask all his colleagues at the magazine to send in applications, not only for themselves, but for each member of their families, too; luckily in this way he managed to get a ticket.

A lot of children would be making the trip on their own, and when Tsuyama reached the platform, he found it crowded with relatives who had come to see them off. The train was already standing at the platform: twelve sleeping cars, painted in their distinctive blue, and a generator car humming contentedly to itself at the front. The locomotive had yet to arrive.

He took out his ticket and looked at it.

"I am at number twelve in the third carriage on the top bunk. I hope there will be a beautiful, young girl in the bunk below me," he said with a mischievous smile at Yukiko.

"Don't you men ever think of anything else?"

"What do you mean? Surely you must agree that you would find a trip much more enjoyable if you could spend it sitting next to a handsome young man?"

"Not at all, I wouldn't care what he looked like as long as he was clever and kind."

"Thank you."

"What?"

"I take it you were referring to me, weren't you?"

Yukiko laughed. Although nobody at the office knew it yet, they were engaged to be married the following spring.

They came to car number three and Tsuyama went in with his luggage. He returned a few minutes later with just his camera hanging from his shoulder.

"Well, I was right about there being a beautiful, young girl in the other berth, the only problem is that she is only about twelve years old!" he said, laughing again.

2

At eleven-forty the type-EF sixty-five locomotive that was to pull the train drew into the station and all the children ran to the end of the platform to get a picture of it.

The following notice was hanging from a pillar by the locomotive:

NOTICE

When photographing,
1. Do not enter the tracks.
2. Do not cross the blue line.
3. Do not run along the platform.
4. Do not enter any areas that are prohibited.
5. Follow the directions of the station personnel.

Non-adherence to the above rules will result in banning of all photographs.

None of the children had time to bother with this, however; they were only interested in getting a picture of the locomotive that was going to pull their train. Tsuyama followed the children at a more leisurely pace and also took a photograph of the front of the train. It was painted the same deep blue as the coaches, with the upper half of the nose a light orange; it was the distinctive coloring that distinguishes the night expresses in Japan. There was a large sign affixed to the front of the train in the shape of a question mark that said "Mystery Train" and obviously some time had been spent making it.

"Go and stand next to the train so I can take your picture," Yukiko said, looking through the viewfinder of her own camera.

Tsuyama went over to the train and held a pose.

"I hope you did not cut my head off this time!" he said teasingly. There was still about fifteen minutes before the train was due to leave, so he lit a cigarette.

"I know it is a Mystery Train, but where do you think it is going?" Yukiko asked. Usually the train's destination was written in a small window on the sides of the carriages, but on the Mystery Train this had been left blank.

"I don't know, but after studying the timetable, I think I have a fair idea." He looked very confident.

"The timetable? What do you mean?"

"Look, I will show you," he said, taking out his dog-eared copy and opening it to the page for the Tokaido line. Yukiko peered over his shoulder.

"Here it is, the 'Milky Way No. 53' leaves Tokyo at eleven fifty-nine, which is the same time as the Mystery Train, and it leaves from the same platform, too."

"But the Milky Way is a special train."

"Yes, it says so here, it only runs on September the eleventh. But what I am trying to say is that instead of making a brand-new schedule for this train, it would be much easier for them just to use the schedule of another train that won't be running today."

"So you think it will be going to Kyoto then? That is where it says the Milky Way goes."

"Yes, I don't think there is any doubt about it," Tsuyama said confidently.

"But the Milky Way is not a sleeper, it says that it is a normal express, while the Mystery Train is a blue train—maybe their destinations are different, too."

While they were still discussing the train's destination a young couple nearby were busy saying farewell to their young son.

". . . And if you have any problems, get in touch with the conductor, he will help you," the mother said.

"Have a good time, son," added the father.

"Look, it's the actor, Ko Nishimoto," Yukiko said to Tsuyama in a low voice.

Now that she had mentioned it, he saw that the young father was indeed the actor who was presently one of the most popular men in the country. The boy resembled him quite closely, especially around the eyes, and Tsuyama realized that with four hundred passengers on the train, there would probably be more famous people or their families on board. He turned his camera on the group and released the shutter; if he had a little piece about the celebrities on the train, it would make his story that much more interesting.

3

"The Mystery Train will be leaving shortly; anyone not holding a valid ticket please leave the train immediately."

Some of the children who had come to the station to see their older brothers and sisters off had climbed on board and were playing in the bunks. Tsuyama stood by the door and talked with Yukiko.

"Give the editor my regards and tell him that I will start writing the story as soon as I get back."

The editor always complained that he was late in handing in his stories after he had been somewhere on a job.

The minute hand on the clock moved up to fifty-nine and the station bell started to ring. The doors slid closed with a bang and Tsuyama only just managed to pull his head in in time. However, the doors soon opened again, and this time they seemed to show no sign of closing.

"I wonder what the problem is?" he said in a loud voice.

"I don't know; there doesn't appear to be anything wrong."

"I know this is supposed to be a Mystery Train, but I don't think it is really necessary to make even the departure time a mystery!" Tsuyama said with a laugh. At that moment a man in a conductor's uniform came running up the stairs with a large parcel under his arm and jumped into the conductor compartment on the seventh coach.

Several of the people who had been watching nearby broke out into laughter as if there had been something very humorous about the way he scurried over to the train and dived in through the open door.

"It looks as if you almost left without one of your conductors," Yukiko said with a smile.

"Yes, I don't know what the railways are coming to. We will have to . . ." Yukiko would never know what he had been about to say because at that moment the doors closed. Tsuyama looked so disappointed at not having been able to finish complaining that she had to struggle to suppress a laugh.

The train started to move and she waved gaily to him. It picked up speed and she watched as it left the station, the red taillight disappearing into the night. Suddenly she felt that the train and its passengers really had disappeared, and she hurriedly turned away. She could not understand why she should feel like this, maybe it was because she was still not quite sure of her relationship with Tsuyama, even though they planned to be married. Then again, it may be because the train was a Mystery Train, but that was silly. The passengers may not know where they were going, but the people at J.N.R. all knew, and the train would be back in Tokyo in two days.

She looked around and realized that all the other people who had come to see the train off had already gone and she was left there on her own. It was now about fifteen minutes past twelve, the Mystery Train had left the station five or six minutes behind schedule, and so it was the ninth of August before it finally got under way.

"Typical of a Mystery Train," she murmured to herself. She realized how silly it was to think the train might actually disappear, after all, it was only a train, and unless it sprouted wings it would have to stay on the tracks; it would be an easy thing for J.N.R. to get in touch with it whenever they wanted.

Tsuyama had promised to telephone her and tell her where he was as soon as the train made its first stop, and he was a man who kept his promises. She knew she could rely on him to call her the next day, or rather later that morning, and she could almost hear him now. "It is just like I said, the first stop was Kyoto!"

It was almost one o'clock by the time she got back to her small apartment in Yotsuya, and it was so hot that she went to bed with the electric fan on. As a result, when she woke up the next morning, she found that she had the beginnings of a cold.

4

It was Sunday and she did not have to go into work.

Yukiko usually stayed in bed until noon on her days off, but a fragment of the unease she had felt the night before still remained with her and she could not sleep. She got up and had a simple breakfast of milk and toast and by the time she had finished, it was still only nine o'clock.

She remembered Tsuyama saying that the Mystery Train would probably run on the same schedule as the Milky Way, and looking it up in her copy of the timetable, she saw that it was due to arrive in Kyoto at nine twenty-five. If he was right and they did run on the same schedule, he would soon be pulling into Kyoto Station and she could expect to hear from him shortly.

She glanced repeatedly at the clock as she sat thinking about various things, and even though the minute hand had passed the six the phone on top of the table remained mute. Soon it was ten o'clock and still there was no word from him. She had always been looked upon as a clever, unflappable person, but she was finding it harder and harder to remain calm. She realized that while being in love was a wonderful thing, it also had its bad sides and worry was one of them.

She tried to tell herself that there was nothing to worry about; she did not know for sure that the train would be headed for Kyoto, she only had Tsuyama's guess to go on. In fact, she had to admit that it would be a little boring if it were just to go to Kyoto and back. It would be much more likely to keep on running all morning and maybe even go as far as Kyushu. Although there was not a buffet car on the train, the train could stop to pick up food at stations along the way, which would appeal to the railway fans who were on board. If that was the case it would be impossible for Tsuyama to get to a phone, the bullet train had a pay phone on board but the blue trains didn't.

Even if the train's destination had been Kyoto, there may have been a tight schedule that did not allow him time to get to a phone or they may even have been asked not to call anyone until they returned to Tokyo; after all, it was supposed to be a Mystery Train. Then, too, Tsuyama was always a very unprepared man and maybe he got to the phone only to realize that he did not have any change and by the time he had managed to get some from a kiosk the train had moved on. She would not put it past him.

No matter how many reasons she thought of to explain why she had received no phone call, she could not convince herself, and at twelve o'clock she decided to telephone and find out if everything was okay. She wondered if she should call the J.N.R. office or Tokyo Station. Remembering that it was Sunday, she realized that the office would be closed. She dialed one hundred four to get inquiries, but no matter how many times she tried, the line was busy. She finally decided that she may as well go to the station and find out for herself since she would not be able to relax at home.

5

She turned the television on as she was getting ready to go out because she wanted to see the twelve o'clock news. She wondered if there had been an accident or something that would cause the train to be delayed.

The newscaster announced that the naked body of a man had been found in the Tama River to the west of Tokyo. It was thought, the reporter said, that because of the intense heat the man had gone for a swim, but that the sudden cold had caused him to have a heart attack, which led to his death. The previous day, twenty-eight people around the country had died in swimming accidents. There was no news of a rail accident anywhere. The news was followed by an amateur singing program that had been running for years, but Yukiko was not there to listen to it.

The heat outside was enough to make her feel dizzy, the midsummer sun blazing out of a cloudless sky without mercy.

It would be nice to go down to Okinawa for a holiday with Tsuyama after he gets back, she thought as she walked toward the subway station.

When she arrived at Tokyo Station, she wondered where she should go to make inquiries and decided that she would just go to the ticket window.

"The Mystery Train?" the man behind the window said in an uninterested tone. "We don't deal with special trains at this window. You'll have to try somewhere else."

"No, you don't understand. I am inquiring about the destination of the Mystery Train that left this station last night."

"I can't tell you that, it would not be a Mystery Train if we went around telling everyone its destination, now would it?" the man said with a malicious grin.

"Be serious, will you?" she said losing her temper.

"I am being serious," he said becoming surly. "Anyway, I am busy, please go and ask somewhere else."

"But where should I ask? That is all I want to know."

"I don't know. Hey, who did that Mystery Train yesterday?" he asked one of his colleagues.

"Oh, that? Osaka."

"That was Osaka, so nobody here will be able to help you, miss."

"What was Osaka?" Yukiko asked, struggling to control her temper.

"That Mystery Train was organized by the Osaka office, so nobody here knows anything about it."

"But it left from this station, surely someone here must know something about it."

Yukiko was not about to give up that easily. She did not care who had planned the Mystery Train originally; as far as she was concerned, it was all the same railway and someone here should be able to help her. It was starting to develop into an argument when one of the deputy stationmasters came over to see what the trouble was.

There are fifty-six deputy stationmasters employed at Tokyo Station, and as luck would have it, the one that appeared had been interviewed by Yukiko a short while before.

"I say, aren't you that reporter from *Ryoso*?" he asked, and Yukiko was very relieved that he had recognized her. As far as she could remember, his name was Aoki.

"Am I glad you're here."

"Why? What seems to be the problem?"

"I am trying to find out where the Mystery Train that left here last night is traveling right now."

"Oh, is it for a story?" he asked with a grin. When Yukiko had interviewed him the previous summer in connection with the story she was writing, "A Day at Tokyo Station," he had been able to tell her all kinds of interesting stories.

"Yes, I'm here on a job."

Although that was not exactly true, she thought it would be easier if she said she was. Anyway, Tsuyama was on the train in order to write a story.

"In that case, please come with me," he said and led her into a reception room next to the stationmaster's office. The walls were covered with photographs of all the stationmasters who had been employed at Tokyo Station since it first opened, and the whole room had quite an antique feel about it.

"The truth is that one of our reporters is on the Mystery Train," Yukiko said, taking a sip of the barley water he had given her, "and he was supposed to call in at the first stop he made. We are in a hurry for the story and I wondered what had happened."

"You mean whether there had been an accident or something?"

"Yes."

"Well, we have not had any news of an accident. Its first destination was Kyoto, but I am afraid that I do not know the details, it was planned by the Osaka office, you see."

"So Kyoto was the first destination then?"

"Yes, I know that it is not very original, but the plan was for them to see the steam locomotives at Umekoji. There is a steam museum there that is very popular with railway enthusiasts."

"What time were they due to arrive there?"

"Well, they left at midnight last night, so they should have reached Umekoji at about ten o'clock or so."

"Are you sure that they actually arrived there?"

Aoki laughed.

"Of course they went there, if that is what their schedule

says, that is where they went, but if you are still worried, I will call and check."

He stood up and walked over to the telephone in the corner of the room.

6

Aoki walked back to her, still smiling.

"As I said, they went there all right. They arrived at ten o'clock and stayed for one hour before moving on."

"A whole hour?"

In that case, what reason could Tsuyama give for not having called her? Aoki, however, misunderstood her concern.

"Yes, everyday, one of the locomotives puts on a display and they waited to watch it before they left."

"Aren't there any pay phones at the museum?"

"Pay phones?" Aoki asked in surprise.

"Yes, pay phones. Aren't there any phones there?"

"Well, we get a lot of visitors at the museum so there are several kiosks, and I am sure that there must be a certain number of phones, too."

If there were phones, why hadn't Tsuyama called her? If he did not have any change he could have got some from the kiosks. If they were there for a whole hour, he could not claim that he did not have the time to call her. Whenever she went on a trip, she always called him as soon as she arrived; after all, that was what being in love was supposed to be all about. She felt a fool for having bothered to worry about him, and her anxiety turned to anger.

"Where are they scheduled to stop after Umekoji?" she asked. She felt that she may as well find out while she was there, perhaps Tsuyama would call her from the next stop.

"I'm afraid I do not know. Would you like me to call the Osaka office and find out?"

"If it is not too much trouble."

"Not at all, after all, it's part of my job."

This time his call took a little longer and when he hung up about fifteen minutes later, the smile was gone from his face.

"That's strange," he said, shaking his head. "The Mystery Train was supposed to change locomotives from electric to diesel in order to make a trip to Tottori, as the San-in line has not been electrified yet."

"And where will they go after Tottori?"

"They are supposed to take the Inbi line down to Okayama and then head straight back to Tokyo. The plan allows for them to get off at Tottori to visit the sand dunes there."

"But why did you say it was strange?"

"Well, according to their schedule, it should have already passed Fukuchiyama Station, but the staff there say they have not seen it yet."

"But if it is not a regular train, maybe they did not notice when it passed. It doesn't stop there, does it?"

"No, you are probably right."

He looked at his watch and Yukiko did the same.

"It is two o'clock now, what time are they due to arrive at Tottori?" she asked.

"At five past three."

"Well, in that case, why don't we just wait and see?"

Time passed and then Aoki went and picked up the phone again. This time the call lasted even longer than the previous one and it was three-thirty before he put down the receiver.

"The Mystery Train has not arrived in Tottori—it has disappeared somewhere," he said.

7

Aoki was not the only one to feel confused, the staff of Tottori Station could not understand it either.

It was only a fifteen-minute drive to the sand dunes from the station, and although there was a regular bus service, it would not be able to cope with the four hundred people who would be arriving on the Mystery Train, so J.N.R. had arranged for eight air-conditioned, fifty-seat buses to be waiting in front of the station.

Although Tottori city is the prefectural capital, it cannot compare with the nearby city of Yonago for industry. Its main source of income is the tourists who are attracted there to see the famous sand dunes, and the arrival of four hundred visitors on the Mystery Train was considered important enough for "Miss Sand Dunes" to be called out to the station to greet them.

The time of the train's arrival—15:05—came and went, and soon it was 15:30, but still there was no sign of it. Tottori had a call from Tokyo asking after it, which only added to their confusion, but they had not been notified of an accident anywhere on the line, so they did not give up the hope that it would arrive eventually.

However, a short while after four o'clock, the Matsukaze No. 3 express arrived in the station and the whole situation took a sudden change for the worse. The Matsukaze No. 3 was an express that ran between Osaka and Tottori and it used the San-in line from Fukuchiyama, which meant it had come on the same route that the Mystery Train was supposed to and yet it was supposed to arrive after the Mystery Train. This could only mean one thing: somewhere along the line the Mystery Train and its four hundred passengers had disappeared into thin air!

Miss Sand Dunes complained that she did not feel very well and went to lie down in the stationmaster's office. Meanwhile, the stationmaster told his assistant, Abe, to find out what had happened to the train. Abe had worked for the railway for twenty-five years and had turned fifty on the seventeenth of the previous month, but in all his years as a railroad man, he had never heard of anything like this ever happening before. A locomotive and twelve carriages could not just disappear like that. Each carriage was approximately sixty-seven-feet long, which came to eight hundred and twenty feet. And then there was the generator car, which meant the train was eight hundred and thirty feet long altogether. He just could not believe something of that size could vanish like that, not to mention the four hundred passengers it was supposed to have been carrying at the time.

At least everything else was quiet. If there had been an accident and the San-in line had been blocked, it would have been terrible with countless calls from passengers and their relatives and all the staff called out to try and get things running again as soon as possible. As it was, however, everything was peaceful and the Matsukaze No. 4 express was about to leave on its journey back to Osaka.

Abe looked at his pocket watch and saw with satisfaction that it left the station exactly on time. Everything was just as usual, except, that is, for the fact that a train full of people had disappeared.

A shudder ran down his spine and all of a sudden he began to feel frightened.

8

If a group of armed men had hijacked the train and forced it to go where they ordered, the whole rail network would be in a state of crisis, but at least they would know what had happened and where the train was. But apart from the disappearance of the train, everything was running as usual; there were no screams or shots ringing out over the tracks.

If he had not been ordered to look into the disappearance by the stationmaster, Abe would probably have just carried on the rest of the day as if nothing had happened. He kept telling himself that something terrible had occurred, but somehow it did not ring true, everything seemed to belie the fact. Miss Sand

Dunes had given up and returned home, but the buses were still waiting outside the station, their drivers chatting together or reading magazines.

The stationmaster had told Abe to find out what had happened to the train, but he did not know where to start. He wondered if the train had really left Tokyo the night before, because if it had, surely it would still be running on schedule. Everything in his twenty-five years of experience made him want to believe that, but the fact that one of the deputy stationmasters from Tokyo had called him to see if the train had arrived would seem to indicate that it had not. The train trip had been planned by the Osaka office, so he thought he had better phone them and see if they could help. Tottori fell under the jurisdiction of the Yonago Branch office, and although there was not any real rivalry between the different offices, the fact that it was another office's problem meant that he did not feel the same urgency he would have otherwise.

He guessed that Osaka would be in a panic, looking for the train, but the person who answered the phone did not sound very upset.

"Tottori? What can I do for you?"

"I am assistant stationmaster Abe . . ." He was so surprised at the other's calmness that he could not think of anything else to say for a moment. "I am phoning about the Mystery Train, I wonder if you could put me through to someone who could help me."

"My name is Ikeda, what can I do for you? I was one of the people involved in the project." He still spoke brightly, as if nothing had happened.

Abe felt very perplexed and did not quite know how to continue.

"Is the Mystery Train running on schedule?"

"Of course. We had a similar query from Tokyo at lunchtime so we checked up on it; everything is going exactly on schedule. They were scheduled to make their first stop at Kyoto where the passengers would go to see the steam museum at Umekoji. I checked with the museum and they confirmed that the group arrived at ten o'clock and stayed to watch a demonstration by a D-fifty-one-type steam locomotive before leaving again at eleven o'clock as planned. They should have arrived at Tottori at fifteen oh five. Did you arrange for the buses to take them to the sand dunes as we requested?"

"Yes, we ordered eight large buses, but the Mystery Train never arrived, so they are still waiting."

"You mean that it didn't arrive at fifteen oh five?"

"I mean that it is now seventeen-twenty and it still has not arrived."

"That's strange." There was a pause for a moment. "They must have had an accident somewhere. You have not heard anything, have you?"

He still seemed to be having trouble grasping the situation and was thinking out loud rather than actually asking a question.

"No, not a word. The San-in line is operating right on schedule."

"Then it cannot have been an accident, but if the other trains are running according to schedule, then surely the Mystery Train must also be running on time."

"I don't know about that, all I know is that it never arrived here. To be quite honest, apart from the buses we have kept waiting, it does not really affect us very much. But considering a whole train has disappeared, I think it might be a good idea if you were to check up on it."

"If what you say is true, then this is a disaster. You are quite sure, are you, that it never arrived at Tottori?"

He still could not believe what had happened.

"Yes, I am quite sure, more than two hours have passed since it was due, but it still has not shown up."

So saying, he hung up the phone.

9

Abe told the stationmaster everything that was said.

"He did not seem to be particularly worried," he added.

"You cannot really blame him for that. As long as there has not been an accident reported, everyone just assumes that things are running according to schedule, it is a kind of overconfidence that all railwaymen share."

"What should we do meanwhile?"

"I don't think there is anything that we *can* do. We will just have to wait until we hear the results of the Osaka office's investigation. What is the time now?"

"Almost six o'clock."

"In that case, I think you had better send the buses back."

"Okay," Abe said, and at that moment the phone rang. Abe was nearest to it and picked up the receiver.

"Is this the Tottori stationmaster's office?" asked a young woman's voice.

"That is correct."

"This is the director's secretary's office, I am putting you through now."

"The director's secretary?"

Abe hurriedly handed the phone to his superior. This was the first time that the secretary to the director of J.N.R. had ever called here.

"Hello, my name is Kitano, I am secretary to the director," said a man's voice.

"This is the Tottori stationmaster speaking. What can I do for you?" he asked tersely. He could not guess what the call could be about; they had no particular problems at his station at the moment.

"I am calling about the Mystery Train that was planned by the Osaka office. I heard that it had not arrived at your station yet, is that true?"

"Yes, it was supposed to have arrived three hours ago and the passengers gone to visit the sand dunes by bus, but it still has not arrived."

"You are quite sure that it has not arrived?"

"Yes, is there a relative of yours on the train or something?"

The stationmaster could not understand why he would be so worried otherwise.

"No, that is not it at all," Kitano said and hung up.

Abe and the stationmaster exchanged a glance.

"What was all that about?"

10

Hiroshi Kitano put the phone down and turned to the director of J.N.R.

"It would appear that it is true."

"We are talking about a twelve-car train, you know? Eight hundred and thirty feet of train doesn't just disappear like that. There are four hundred passengers, too."

"But it is certain that it never arrived at Tottori. It would appear that the man on the phone was speaking the truth."

"But is it possible for a whole train to vanish like that? Couldn't it have just broken down somewhere, and that the man saw it and called us up as a prank?"

"I suppose it is a possibility, but if that was so, surely the whole timetable would be interrupted, yet the other trains on both the Tokaido line and the San-in line are all running to the minute. That can only mean that the Mystery Train is not on the tracks on either of those lines."

"Yes, that is true." Kimoto gave a small groan. The pipe in his hand had gone out some minutes ago, but he did not seem to notice.

"What should we do?"

Kimoto thought about it for a while before he answered.

"There are too many people's lives at stake; we can't ignore it. You had better call the police."

"Who should I ask for?"

"How about that officer in the investigation section who helped us with that last case. What was his name . . . ? Inspector Totsugawa."

"What should I say? Shall I just ask him to come over?"

"Tell him that there has been a kidnapping on one of our trains. Tell him that four hundred, no, we must not forget our own people, you had better make that four hundred and six. Tell him that four hundred and six people have been kidnapped."

"Should I tell him about the Mystery Train?"

"No, that can wait until he gets here. The important thing is to get him here as soon as possible. I'm sure he will be able to help us."

Having said this he seemed to realize for the first time that his pipe had gone out and picked up his matches to relight it.

THE RANSOM

1

When he had first heard that four hundred people had been kidnapped, Totsugawa could not quite grasp the enormity of the situation. Four hundred people was simply too many for a kidnapping, and he just could not understand what Kitano meant when he said that a whole train had disappeared. One thing he did notice, though: Kitano was panic-stricken. He had only met the man once before, and then he had seemed a picture of normality, a man who knew his own limitations and would be the last to panic. However, this time Kitano was very obviously close to panicking, which only underlined the seriousness of the disaster that had overtaken the railways.

Totsugawa and his superior, Detective Sergeant Honda, hurried over to the J.N.R. head office to see what it was all about.

"What do they mean when they say that a train has disappeared and all the passengers have been kidnapped?" Honda asked Totsugawa as they got into the elevator together.

"I can't understand it myself, but they seem to be serious. The director of J.N.R. is going to talk to us in person."

"Well, I hope it turns out to be an open and shut case."

Kitano was waiting for them outside the director's office and he showed them straight in as soon as they arrived.

"Please take a seat," Kimoto said when they entered.

"Do you mind if I smoke?" Totsugawa asked, taking out his cigarettes.

"Not at all, go ahead, I always think better myself when I can smoke my pipe." So saying, he picked up his briar and clenched it between his teeth, but he did not light it.

"We heard something about a kidnapping," Honda said.

"Yes, I had a phone call about an hour ago—one hour and thirteen minutes ago to be precise. My secretary Kitano took the call."

He glanced over at Kitano.

"It was a man's voice," Kitano said, taking up the story.

"And what did this man have to say?"

"He told me to put the director on the line. When I told him that he would have to tell me his business first, he said that he had kidnapped the passengers of the Mystery Train and demanded that we pay a ransom to get them back."

"Oh, I read about that train in the papers. Its destination was secret, but it was very popular."

"Yes, it was a twelve-coach sleeper that left Tokyo Station last night with four hundred passengers on board. As you say, although nobody knew its destination, it was very popular and we had eight thousand applications for it. Anyway, at first I thought it was just a hoax, but it was too important to ignore so I decided to discuss it with the director."

"I took the call from him," Kimoto said.

"What did the man say to you?" Honda asked.

"He told me the same thing. He said that he had kidnapped the four hundred passengers of the Mystery Train and he demanded one billion yen in ransom."

"One billion?"

"Yes, he said that at only two and a half million each, it was very cheap. Of course, at that time I still did not believe the Mystery Train had disappeared and I told him as much."

"What did he say to that?"

"He just laughed."

2

Kimoto's face flushed at the memory.

"He just laughed and said that if I did not believe him, I should check and see where the Mystery Train was right now. He said that he would call me back and then he hung up."

"Did you check?"

"Yes, I did," Kitano said. "The Mystery Train was planned by the Osaka office so first I called them, but they seemed to think it was running according to schedule. It was supposed to stop at Kyoto first to allow the passengers to visit the steam museum at Umekoji. When they checked there, they were told that the visitors had arrived on schedule. I was very relieved to hear this, but I thought I would check at the next stop, Tottori, just to make sure. The plan called for them to stop there at five past three and to stay for an hour so that the passengers could visit the sand dunes. It was after six when I called and they informed me that although the Mystery Train had yet to arrive, the Matsukaze express, which was supposed to have followed it, had already arrived."

"In other words, the Mystery Train has disappeared," Totsugawa said.

"I am afraid that it is the only explanation," Kitano answered, looking pale and biting his lip.

Honda looked at his watch. It was a little after seven o'clock.

"You said that the man was going to call you back later, didn't you?" he asked Kimoto.

"Yes, that is correct."

"In that case, we should be ready for him."

Totsugawa connected the tape recorder he had brought with him to the telephone so it would automatically record any incoming calls.

The tension in the room grew until it seemed hard to breathe.

"He must be mad to expect that much money," Honda said with a smile in an effort to make them relax.

"Yes, he said that it was two and a half million per person," Kimoto said in disgust, repeating what had already been said. "He is a sarcastic villain if nothing else."

"What do you mean, sarcastic?"

"The railway's annual debt is now up to one trillion per year and it employs approximately four hundred thousand people."

"I see, so you mean that the annual debt comes to two and a half million yen per person."

"Exactly. It is as if each worker is being given two and a half million yen from the government every year. It is very humiliating for me as the director of the corporation."

"Do you think the kidnapper knew this and that was why he decided to charge the same ransom for the hostages?"

"I think so."

At that moment the quiet in the room was shattered by the sudden ringing of the phone.

Kimoto's expression froze with shock and he looked aghast at the offending instrument. Kitano picked up the receiver and the tape started to turn.

"Yes, the director's office."

"Oh, you are that secretary, aren't you? Put me through to the director."

It was a man's voice.

Kitano looked toward the director to see what he wanted to do.

"I'll take it," he said and took the receiver.

"This is Kimoto speaking."

"Did you find your Mystery Train? How about its passengers?"

"What have you done with them? Send them back immediately."

"If you give me one billion yen in ransom the passengers can go home safely."

"What if I refuse?"

"You will never see those four hundred people again—or if you do, it will be as corpses. If that happens, J.N.R. will be held responsible and it will cost you a lot more than a billion yen before the relatives are finished with you."

The man's voice took on a threatening tone.

"Okay," Kimoto said and hung his head.

"Well, as long as we know where we both stand. It is seven-thirty now. I want you to get the money ready by nine o'clock."

"That is impossible. Today is Sunday. I cannot get my hands on that kind of money until the banks open tomorrow."

"Don't give me that, you represent the Japanese National Railways. Get the money together by nine o'clock or you can forget about ever seeing the four hundred people again. But no, it is not merely four hundred, I was forgetting, we've got six of your men, too."

"But it is impossible, I can't manage it by nine o'clock!"

"I will call you again at nine o'clock," the man said and the line went dead.

"Shit!" the director said, using a word nobody had ever heard him use before.

"What are you going to do?" Kitano asked.

"Well, I cannot go to the banks until tomorrow. So I suppose I don't have any choice but to go and discuss this with the minister of transport and see what he recommends."

So saying he stood and left the room.

3

Kimoto met with the minister of transport and it was arranged that the Bank of Japan would loan the necessary money to the railroad. By the time he got back to his office it was eight-fifty.

"Thank goodness I was able to get back in time," he said, looking relieved and wiping the perspiration from his face with a handkerchief.

"Do you intend to pay?" Honda asked.

"I don't think we have any option, do we?" Kimoto answered irritably.

"No, I suppose not."

"Ever since the prime minister first asked me to take over as director of J.N.R., my one aim has been to try and ensure that there were no major accidents while I was in charge. Sometimes I even wake up in the middle of the night, having dreamt that there had been an accident, but so far nothing has happened. In the past, whenever there has been a major accident, the director was forced to resign. Don't get me wrong, it is not my job that I am worried about, it is the thought of all the lives that may be lost if something were to go wrong. Well, now the lives of four hundred passengers and six railway employees are in danger and I intend to do everything in my power to ensure that nothing happens to them."

Hearing this, the police realized that they would not be able to stop him from paying the ransom even if they wanted to.

"There is one more thing," Kimoto said.

"What is that?"

"I want you to keep your inquiries under the tightest secrecy. If the kidnappers find out that the police are involved with the case, they may kill the hostages anyway."

"That is all right with us, but the problem is that even

though we carry out our inquiries in secret, the press and the passengers' relatives are going to make a lot of fuss if the train does not return to Tokyo Station on schedule."

"Exactly. That is why I want you to get all the hostages back by the time the train is due to return."

"What time is that?"

"It is due back at nine-thirty tomorrow morning."

"Nine-thirty tomorrow? Well, it is nine o'clock now, so we have just over twelve hours in which to rescue them."

"We could probably say that the train was delayed and put them off until about eleven o'clock tomorrow morning," Kitano said.

That still only left fourteen hours; would that be sufficient time to rescue the hostages and arrest the kidnappers?

The fact that nobody knew the train's ultimate destination or where it would stop along the way was one of the reasons for its immense popularity, but that same fact would have played right into the hands of the kidnappers, Totsugawa thought. No matter where the train might be taken or how strange the place where it stopped, nobody would question it. They would just assume that it was another attraction. But all the same, how could they make a whole train disappear like that, and what had happened to all the passengers? He tried to visualize it. The train itself was over eight hundred feet long with an electric locomotive coupled to one end, and no matter where it went, it had to remain on the rails. He was still trying to figure out if there really was a way of making something that big disappear when the phone rang. He glanced over at the phone and then he looked at his watch.

It was exactly nine o'clock.

4

At least he's punctual, he thought.

This time Kimoto answered the phone himself.

"Hello, Kimoto speaking."

"Have you got the money ready?" the man asked.

"I am still organizing it," Kimoto said.

"I thought I told you to have it ready by nine o'clock," the man said in an angry tone.

Kimoto frowned.

"We are doing our best, but a billion yen is a lot of money and with the banks closed we can't just go and pick it up. We need another hour."

From the man's manner up until then Kimoto thought that he would lose his temper, but the kidnapper answered quite calmly.

"If I wait until ten o'clock are you sure you will have the money together?"

"I think so."

"Okay, I will give you until ten o'clock then, but if I find that the police have been called in, the deal's off. And I don't want you to try any clever tricks either."

"Just a minute . . ."

"If this is just a trick to try and stretch out the conversation, you can just forget it."

"No, but I need assurance that the passengers are all safe. As director of J.N.R. I have a responsibility to all the passengers and all the more so if I am to pay a billion yen to have them released."

"You can do what you like."

The man sounded indifferent, and this only served to make him all the more terrible.

"What do you mean?"

"Do you honestly expect me to bring all four hundred people to the phone so you can talk to them? You have got to be joking. Either you pay me the sum I have asked for or tomorrow you will find a train full of corpses heading up the Tokaido line. It is all the same to me."

Totsugawa was listening to the conversation on an extension

and he felt that the threat in the other man's voice was real. Kimoto also felt the same and spoke quickly.

"Okay, I understand, I will have the money ready by ten o'clock."

"Now you are being sensible," the man said and hung up.

"So we have another hour," Kimoto said, looking at the clock.

"Will you really be able to get the money ready by then?" Honda asked.

Kimoto smiled.

"The bank promised that they would have it ready by nine o'clock, but I didn't like his attitude. I don't see why he should have everything his way."

"You also managed to win us an extra hour," Kitano said. Totsugawa, however, shook his head.

"I don't think so, I think they had already planned for such a delay."

"Why do you say that?" Kimoto asked, looking up sharply.

"I think we are dealing with a very calculating yet demanding man. He demonstrated this when you asked for proof that the hostages were safe by simply telling you that if you did not do just what he told you, you would find a train full of corpses. However, when you told him that you would need another hour to gather the money, he agreed without a comment."

"But if I cannot get the money together, he will be the one who loses."

"I am afraid that I cannot agree. He is a very high-handed man, but he agreed to lengthen the time limit without so much as a murmur of protest. I believe he had planned for you to hand over the money at ten o'clock all along."

"If that is true, what could it mean?"

Totsugawa thought for a few minutes.

"I must admit that I cannot understand that either. In a kidnapping case, the police have the best chance of arresting the kidnappers when they come to collect the ransom, as that is the only time they have to come out into the open."

"Yes, I can see that."

"Picking up the ransom is where the kidnappers have to use their heads. The easiest way is to have the money taken to a preselected spot and left there, but that allows the police to stake the place out and it has little chance of success. Criminals who are slightly more clever will tell the victim's relatives to take the money on a light plane, train, or car and then suddenly tell them when to throw it out. This means that the police are unable to set a trap, but if the person who delivers the money has a radio transmitter with him, he can tip the police off straight away, which often leads to an arrest. In this case, the kidnapper has told you to have the money ready by ten o'clock, and I think that has some connection with the method they intend to use to collect it."

"Have you got any ideas?"

"No, I am afraid I don't, but as soon as we know a little more, we will be able to do something."

"How much does a billion yen weigh?" Kitano asked.

"If I remember rightly, a hundred million weighs almost thirty pounds, so a billion yen will weigh about three hundred pounds."

"It's not as heavy as I thought it would be."

"No, but the problem is the size. It will fill about five suitcases, and so the kidnapper must have thought of some way of carrying it."

Honda looked at his watch and then looked up at the clock on the wall as if to check it. It was nine twenty-seven. There were thirty-three minutes to go, but would they be able to guess the kidnapper's plan by then?

Totsugawa sat deep in thought. From the way the kidnapper spoke, he sounded very confident, although that was only to be expected considering he had managed to hijack a whole train and make it disappear without anyone knowing about it. But was he going to be equally lucky when it came to collecting the ransom?

"Kitano, ring the Osaka office and see what they have been able to learn," Kimoto said.

Totsugawa watched as Kitano walked over to the phone and made the call. If by some miracle the people at the Osaka office had managed to find the train and its passengers, they would not have to worry about paying the ransom at all.

Kitano put the phone down and turned to Kimoto.

"They are still looking for it; they have not been able to come up with anything yet."

"Are they really trying?" Kimoto asked irritably.

Kitano looked at a loss.

"I am sure they are doing all they can."

"I am sorry, it is just that at a time like this, it makes life very difficult when you have to deal with the unions," Kimoto said, voicing one of his pet hates.

The Japanese railways were represented by three main unions and Kimoto and Kitano always had trouble trying to keep all of them happy.

5

The man called again at exactly ten o'clock. Kimoto picked up the receiver and the tape started to run.

He is a very punctual man, Totsugawa thought again.

Sometimes a kidnapper would purposely delay his calls in order to play on the nerves of his victims, but not this one, he kept his promises to the minute. That was one more thing that they now knew about him, he was very confident and he was punctual. It was not a lot to go on but at least it was a start.

"It is ten o'clock," said the man.

"Yes, I know."

"Have you got the money ready?"

"Yes, we can deliver it anytime you say, but first I want some kind of guarantee that you will release the hostages once you get your money."

"You will get the train back, too, I guarantee it, but only if you follow my instructions exactly. If you try any clever tricks, there is no telling what may happen."

"What do you want me to do?"

"I want you to pack the money into bags no bigger than ten inches by thirty. You should be able to get a hundred million in each, which means that you will need ten altogether. When you've done that, I want you to take them to Ueno Station and you had better be there no later than ten forty-five."

"Then what?"

"If you get them to Ueno Station on time, you will find out," he said and hung up.

"Who does he think he is?" Kimoto asked, angrily slamming the phone down.

"We have only forty minutes," Kitano said quietly.

"Okay, you hurry over to the Bank of Japan; I will call them and have them load the money into bags as he described."

"We will go with him," Honda said, and the three of them hurried out of the room.

They drove over to the bank in a station wagon and when they arrived they found that the money had already been packed into sacks of the size dictated by the kidnapper.

"I am afraid that we did not have time to copy down the serial numbers," said the clerk who handed it over.

"That does not matter," Totsugawa said. He knew it would be impossible to check the numbers on all the notes in the brief time available to them, and anyway, he intended to arrest the kidnappers before they had a chance to use any of it.

The clerk helped them load the money into the back of the car.

"I hope you catch these kidnappers and that this money is not added to the railway's debt," he said.

Kitano drove as they hurried along the expressway toward Ueno Station. Luckily it was Sunday night and the traffic was moving smoothly, or they would never have managed to get there in time.

"Have you any idea why he should want us to be at the station by ten forty-five, or why he wanted the sacks to be thirty inches long?" Honda asked from the rear seat.

"I think the time is connected to the departure of a train, but I have no idea why he should have stipulated that the sacks should be this size," Kitano said.

"Maybe he only chose Ueno Station to make us think that he was going to use a train when in fact he plans to get away in a car," Totsugawa suggested.

"Yes, and maybe that was why he said that the bags had to be under thirty inches long, so they could fit into the trunk of a car."

"But if that was the case, he would not need to specify a time. If he came by car, any time would be okay," Honda said thoughtfully.

"That is true," Totsugawa replied, nodding.

The car with its cargo of money pulled into the station at ten forty-three. Totsugawa looked out through the car windows.

"Do you think they are watching us?"

"Nobody followed us here," Honda said.

It was quite possible that the kidnappers had been there waiting for them, and although the car they were driving was unmarked, they could easily know Kitano's face. Kitano got out and went to see if there was a message waiting for them from the director.

"I hope we look like railway men," Totsugawa said.

Kitano still did not return to the car, although it was now past the time limit.

I hope nothing has gone wrong, Totsugawa thought and looked worriedly around the station. It was then that he saw Kitano running back toward the car.

"What happened?" he asked.

"The stationmaster had a call from the kidnappers. We are to put the money on the eleven-oh-five express to Aomori."

"Whereabouts on the train are we supposed to leave it?"

"We're to put it on one of the berths. Now we know why he stipulated that the bags be thirty inches long, if they were any bigger, they would stick out into the corridor. But we must hurry, we don't have much time before the train leaves."

"So we know what the length was for, but how about the width?"

"I am afraid I have no idea."

6

The train was called the Yuzuru No. 13 and was already standing at the platform when they arrived. It was a night express that started from Ueno and arrived in Aomori ten hours and fifty minutes later after traveling along the Joban line. It consisted of eleven coaches, a baggage car, and an electric locomotive.

A lot of the other passengers watched with interest as Kitano, Totsugawa, and Honda walked through the ticket barrier with the long thin bags under their arms. Totsugawa could not help but wonder if the kidnapper was among them.

"Which carriage are we to put the money on?" he asked Kitano.

"We're to put it on bunk number sixteen in the last carriage," Kitano answered without slowing his pace.

This was not entirely true, as the last car was the baggage car, but they were to put it on the last passenger car.

The train consisted of the same type of sleeper cars as the Mystery Train and so it was painted the same deep blue. It seemed hard to believe that such a beautiful train would be involved in a kidnapping.

The chief conductor came out of his office on the platform and gave them a hard look.

"Hey, you! What are you doing?" he asked. They must have looked suspicious hurrying along the platform with their strange load.

"I am the director's secretary," Kitano replied and showed him his I.D. card.

The chief conductor looked surprised for a moment and then said, "What are you going to do with them?"

"I have been ordered to put them on berth sixteen in carriage number one."

"What's inside?"

"I am afraid that I am not at liberty to tell you, but I can assure you that it is nothing dangerous."

"But . . ."

"I guarantee it is nothing dangerous, you have my word on it."

"Yes, I understand, but car number one has been fully booked by a group," he said looking at his schedule.

The two detectives exchanged glances.

"Are you sure?"

"Yes, all thirty-four berths in car number one have been taken."

"Have there been any cancellations?"

"Not so far."

"But that can't be . . ."

The kidnapper had been quite clear when he had said that the money should be left in car one. When the train is bound for Tokyo, car one is at the front, but when it makes its way back to Aomori, it becomes the last car.

There was no more time before the train left.

"Let's go and have a look anyway," Kitano said.

The chief conductor led the way to the car and Kitano went inside. As the conductor had said, it was filled with a group, a lot of them standing in the corridor talking while some had already climbed into their berths and were sipping whiskey from hip flasks or reading magazines. Berth number sixteen was at one end of the carriage and when they got there, they found the curtains open.

Kitano turned to a man in his mid-fifties who was sitting on the opposite bed.

"Do you know whose berth this is?"

"I am pretty sure that it belongs to Mr. Ishiyama," he replied without taking his cigarette from his mouth.

"Has he arrived yet, this Mr. Ishiyama?"

"Now you mention it, I don't think I have seen him."

7

Kitano went back to the door where he had left the other two waiting.

"Bring it on," he said, and had the conductor go back to his office while they carried the bags along the corridor to berth number sixteen.

"Don't worry, we will move it if Mr. Ishiyama turns up," he said to the man sitting opposite.

They loaded the bags onto the bed and it was full with only six of them, the other four had to be piled on top.

"What's in them?" the man asked curiously.

"Just goods for our shop. We work for the head branch and we were told to rush these up to the Aomori Branch by the morning."

"I see."

"What is this group you are all in?"

"It is a travel club called the Nennikai; we are on our way to visit Mount Osore."

"Mount Osore on the Shimokita peninsula?"

"That's right."

"How did you all meet? Do you work for the same company?"

"No. We met through a travel magazine so there are all

kinds of people here, from doctors to schoolteachers. I am a baker myself," he said, and laughed.

"What kind of person is the man who is supposed to have this berth?" Kitano asked.

"Ishiyama? If I remember rightly, I think he said he was an office worker."

"Do you know where he works?" asked Totsugawa.

"He is a chief clerk at a company called Taiyo Manufacturing," said a man's voice from above their heads.

They looked up and saw a round-faced man looking down from the upper bunk.

"If he is a chief clerk, I suppose he must be in his early thirties then."

"I think he is twenty-seven or eight," the man said. At that moment the bell on the platform rang and the loudspeakers announced the train's departure. The train lurched suddenly and then it started to pull silently out of the station.

They closed the curtains on the berth and went to stand in the corridor. They could see the lights of the city slipping past at an ever-increasing pace as the train picked up speed.

"I wonder what the kidnappers intend to do," Kitano said. Honda lit a cigarette before answering.

"I have no idea, but I should think they will get in contact with us before the train reaches Aomori. The train is connected to control center in Tokyo by radio, isn't it?"

"Yes, that is correct."

"In that case I should imagine the kidnapper will telephone the director again and have him pass on their message to us over the radio."

"What do you think they will have us do?"

"I don't know, I can only guess that they will have us throw the money off the train when it passes over a bridge or something."

"But Honda, this is an air-conditioned train; the windows

don't open. The doors won't open either while the train is in motion."

"The window in the rest room opens, doesn't it? I remember seeing a movie called *Heaven and Hell* where the hero throws the bag containing the ransom out of the toilet window."

"It is true that the window in the rest room opens, but only a fraction; it would be impossible to throw a bag of that size through it," Kitano said with a nod toward the bunk.

"In that case the only thing they could do would be to unload it when the train stops at a station somewhere, but that would mean they would be seen by the porters in the station, which does not sound very smart."

"Maybe everyone in this group is a member of the gang," Kitano said, lowering his voice.

"All of them?" Honda looked around in surprise, but then shook his head. "No, I think you're barking up the wrong tree there."

"Why is that?"

"I have never heard of a gang of kidnappers that size before. It would be too hard to organize something like that and there would be much more chance of one of them betraying the others. In a complicated case like this one it would be important for the boss to have absolute control over the others, and that means there aren't likely to be more than ten of them altogether."

8

While Honda and Kitano were talking this over, Totsugawa made a detailed check of the car.

There was a door at both ends, but the one at the rear, which led to the baggage car, was locked. The other door was not locked, but it was already after twelve midnight, and as this car was at the very end of the train nobody was passing through. The large windows on the corridor were all fixed and could not be opened.

It is almost like a locked room in a mystery story, he thought. That was why, of course, the air-conditioning was so efficient. It was in the nineties outside, but inside the train it was almost cold.

The conductor came around and checked the tickets soon after the train left Tokyo, and by the time the train was approaching its first stop, at Mito, all the people who had been standing in the corridor and talking had gone into their bunks and the sound of snores filled the car.

Kitano and the other two, however, could not sleep. Not only did they have the money to guard, but the train was full and there were no vacant bunks that they could use, so they just pulled out the folding seats in the corridor and tried to while away the time.

The train was due to arrive at its first stop at twelve forty-six, and as it did so all three tensed, but nothing happened. All the passengers in car number one were traveling through to Aomori so nobody got up or left the train, and there was no message from the kidnapper. Nine minutes later, the train left the station.

"Why don't they do something?" Kitano asked irritably.

"They are in charge at the moment. We don't have any choice but to wait and see what they want," Totsugawa replied.

"But it is already one o'clock in the morning. If the Mystery Train does not get back to Tokyo in another nine hours, there will be all hell to pay. Not only that, but the Mystery Train disappeared in the west of the country, while this one is heading north. There is something funny going on."

"But the kidnapper told us to load the money on this train, so we don't have any choice but to wait an . . ." his voice slurred and he tried to repeat it. "No choice but to . . ." For some reason he was no longer able to speak properly any more.

What's going on . . . ?

He could not think straight and his eyes started to lose focus.

That smells like chloroform! he thought, realizing what had happened. Someone put chloroform . . .

Someone had put chloroform in the air-conditioning and it had come out through the vent to fill the whole car.

Totsugawa stood up and grabbed the window frame. He knew it would not open, but still he tried with all his strength until he could not fight it any longer and the floor slid up toward him.

9

All he wanted to do was sleep, but somebody was shaking him roughly. Let me sleep! he called out in his dream, but it did no good. Suddenly something cold hit him in the face and shocked him to his senses. It was a wet handkerchief.

"Are you all right?" asked the chief conductor, peering into his face.

"It was the chloroform."

"So that smell was chloroform, was it? I came back from car six and noticed a funny smell in the air and then I saw you all lying in the corridor."

"Where are we now?"

"Well, it is two-fifty so we have just passed Tomioka."

"What, two-fifty?"

They had been asleep for almost two hours. He staggered to his feet, the smell of the chloroform was much weaker now, but his head still felt heavy.

"Look after those two, will you?" he said, pointing to where Honda and Kitano were still lying on the floor. He staggered into the compartment and pushed open the curtains to bunk number sixteen. All the members of the travel club had also been affected by the chloroform and were in a deep sleep.

He stood and looked at the empty bunk and felt the blood drain from his face as he realized that the money had gone.

He turned back to the conductor.

"Has the train stopped anywhere since we left Mito?"

"Yes, we stopped at Taira at two-eleven for six minutes. But it was only a service stop and no passengers got on or off."

"Are you sure? There wasn't anyone who complained of feeling sick and got off?"

"No, we didn't even open the doors on the passenger cars, and anyway, I was standing on the platform the whole time and I did not see anyone leave the train."

"What about after Taira?"

"We have not stopped anywhere else."

If that was the case, there was a good chance that the kidnappers and the money were still on the train.

YUZURU NO. 13

1

The train sped through the night as if nothing had happened. Honda and Kitano were in the washroom splashing water on their faces to try and remove the effects of the chloroform.

"Are you okay?" Totsugawa asked as he walked up to them. He had washed his own face repeatedly, but still his eyes twitched and he had a terrible headache. Honda looked up, rubbing his eyes.

"How about the money, is it safe?"

"It is gone. It would appear that the kidnappers knocked out everyone in this car and then made off with the money."

"We lost them then?"

"Maybe not."

"What do you mean?"

"Well, the train has not made any stops since Mito. To be precise, it made a short stop at Taira at eleven minutes past two, but this was only a service stop to unload some freight and take on fresh water, none of the passenger doors were opened."

"So you mean that they are still on board?" He was still

43

having difficulty in keeping his eyes open, but they suddenly flashed with an inner light.

"Not only that, but the money should still be here somewhere, too. The doors weren't opened and as we discussed earlier, none of the windows can be opened either."

"What do you suggest we do?" Honda asked, both he and Kitano looking up expectantly. Totsugawa turned to the conductor.

"Can you tell us which stations the train will be stopping at after this?"

"Including service stops?"

"Yes."

At that moment there was a loud roar as the Tokyo bound express passed them. The conductor wrote out the following timetable and passed it to Totsugawa.

*3:13	Momouchi	3 mins.
*3:30	Haranomachi	2 mins.
*4:13	Okuma	3 mins.
*4:36	Sendai	2 mins.
5:46	Ichinoseki	2 mins.
6:08	Mizusawa	1 min.
6:23	Kitakami	1 min.
7:00	Morioka	2 mins.
7:58	Ichinohe	30 secs.

*Service stops only.

"This means that none of the passengers can get off the train until it stops at Ichinoseki at five forty-six," Totsugawa said, looking over to the conductor for confirmation. The timetable he received had gone on to list Sannohe, Hachinohe, Misawa, Noheji until finally the train arrived at Aomori at nine fifty-five.

"That is correct," the conductor said, nodding.

"They must have taken the money while we were unconscious and hidden it somewhere else on the train," Kitano said looking toward Totsugawa.

"That is the only possible answer. They must have hidden it in their own beds and are now keeping out of sight until they can unload it later on."

"But those bags weigh thirty pounds each. It would be a lot for one person to carry."

"Yes, but it would be easy for five people. They would only have to carry two bags each. I think it very unlikely that this crime was done by one man; it is much too complicated for that."

"Do you think they are going to wait until the train makes its first passenger stop at Ichinoseki before they try and get the money off?"

"I don't think they have much choice, and in the meantime, we must make our own plans."

2

"But what can we do?" Kitano asked.

The passengers in car number one were still all fast asleep from the effects of the chloroform, but at this time of the morning the majority of passengers on the other cars would also be fast asleep. They could not very well go down the train and wake everyone up in order to search for the money. If they did, there would be chaos on board.

"What time are the beds folded away?" Totsugawa asked the conductor.

"At around seven o'clock."

"Seven o'clock? That is the time the train gets to Morioka, isn't it?"

"Yes, at around that time we fold back the bunks and convert them into seats."

Should they wait until then to start their search? But the train would be making three stops before Morioka, and if they were to lose their prey before they made the search, everything would be lost.

"Can I get in touch with anyone while the train is still moving?" Totsugawa asked the conductor.

"Yes, we can get through to the Tokyo control center by radio."

"Good. I want you to get through to them and have them arrange for some railway police to come on board at the next station."

"How many men should I ask for?"

"Well, there are eleven passenger cars altogether, but luckily each only has one exit, so one man can check all the passengers boarding and leaving at that point. The three of us can cover three cars, which means that we will need another eight."

"We can help, too," said the conductor.

"Thank you, but you and your men also have to look after all the passengers. All the same, we would be very grateful if you could keep your eyes open for anything unusual."

"You can rely on us."

"Thank you. The next stop is at Momouchi, isn't it?"

"Yes, it is only a small station, but they should be able to get the men you need at Haranomachi, which is the next stop after that. If we call them straight away, they should have time to get things organized."

"If they have trouble in getting the men together, you can tell them to call the local police and have them send some men over."

The conductor got through to Tokyo Station without any more delay and asked for the men but without explaining why they were needed. Tokyo got in touch with Haranomachi Station and they quickly arranged for the railway police at the adjacent stations to hurry over in time for the express.

The train stopped at Momouchi for three minutes and then continued on its journey to pull into Haranomachi at three-thirty in the morning.

The platform was brightly lit, but was almost deserted. The only people standing there were a small group of policemen clustered at one end. Totsugawa had the guard open the door in car number one, and he and Honda got out to meet them.

Maybe it was because of the station's proximity to the sea, but there was a cool breeze in the air. From the outside, the train looked like some huge sleeping reptile. All the curtains were closed and it was easy to imagine that everyone aboard was fast asleep, everyone, that is, except for whoever had taken the money. Totsugawa took out his I.D. and showed it to the men waiting there. He did not mention the kidnapping, he merely told them that there may be some men on board who had stolen a large amount of money.

"They have got one billion yen packed in ten, light brown bags, ten inches by thirty. Each bag weighs about thirty pounds, which comes to three hundred pounds altogether."

"So that means there is more than one of them," one of the railway police said tensely.

"Yes, we are fairly sure that there are several of them, but I am afraid we know absolutely nothing about them, not what they look like, their age, or even if they are male or female. You must also bear in mind that they may transfer the money from the bags to suitcases or Boston bags, so keep your eyes open."

"Can we be sure that the men and the money are still on the train?"

"I think so. When the train left Mito Station last night the money still had not disappeared, and it has only made service stops since then. The conductor assures me that none of the passengers got off the train at any of those."

The train made only a two-minute stop at Haranomachi, so there was no time to discuss it any further. They all hurried aboard and the train pulled out of the station without even ringing the station bell. A majority of the passengers on the train would be completely oblivious to the fact that they had ever stopped there.

Totsugawa called them all together in the corridor of car number one and they discussed what they were to do in greater detail before going to take up their positions at the exits to each of the carriages. The train made its stops at Okuma and Sendai but nobody tried to get off. Outside, the night faded and soon the powerful summer sun rose.

At five forty-six the train pulled into Ichinoseki right on schedule and the doors all opened. Totsugawa was on guard in car one, and as all the passengers in that car were booked through to Aomori, nobody got off and nobody tried to get on either. Whether or not it was the effect of the chloroform, all of them were still fast asleep and showed no sign of waking soon.

In all, seventeen people got off at Ichinoseki and the policemen on the doors checked everyone who had any large luggage. There was some trouble, but they told people that they were looking for a bank robber who was thought to be on the train. After that most people were quite cooperative—they did not want anyone to think they had anything to do with the crime.

After a two-minute stop the train resumed its trip, and although the kidnappers may have been among the seventeen people who got off at Ichinoseki, they did not take their money with them. Totsugawa thought it very unlikely that they would have left it on the train after all the trouble they went to in order to get it in the first place.

The train stopped at Mizusawa, Kitakami, and then at seven o'clock precisely it pulled into Morioka. Not only was the time convenient, but because Morioka was the capital city of Iwate Prefecture a lot of passengers got off there. Many of them were on their way to visit relatives and as a result tended to have a lot of luggage. All the luggage was examined but there was still no sign of the money. Seven people boarded the train here. The sleeping berths were folded away at this time, and it was not necessary for them to pay extra for a berth.

Five people who were employed to fold away the berths also came on board. This used to be done by J.N.R. employees, but now the job was farmed out to a private company and the men, all in their twenties, did not waste any time in starting work.

The passengers all went out into the corridor while their compartments were being converted and so it was very easy for the police to use this opportunity to check each one. The men worked very efficiently folding the top berth away into the ceiling and converting the bottom one into a seat. Totsugawa was confident that the money was still on the train somewhere, and that when the beds were folded away it would come to light. Kitano, Totsugawa, Honda, and the eight railway police split into two groups and started from opposite ends of the train. They checked each compartment and opened any suspicious luggage, but they did not find so much as a hundred yen coin. They went through the whole train again, this time with two conductors to help them, but the result was the same. Even if the money had been transferred to another bag, the sacks would still have to be left somewhere. They searched the trash cans and even the rest rooms, but to no avail.

The train would be stopping at Ichinohe any minute.

Have the kidnappers managed to get away with it? Totsugawa thought. A look of impatience clouded his face. "Where can the money have gone?" he muttered, the strain showing in his features.

"We have looked everywhere," Honda replied with a shrug.

The windows were all fixed so the money could not have been disposed of that way, and although the window in the rest room opened, it only moved about four inches. It would have been impossible to force the sacks through. Of course, the kidnappers could have opened the sacks and dropped the money out one million at a time, but not only would that have taken too long, but it would be virtually impossible to collect the money afterward. The train was traveling at over forty miles per hour, and the time needed to drop one thousand wads of bank notes would be prohibitive.

"How about the baggage car?" Honda asked, lowering his voice.

"The luggage car?"

"Yes, if we were to assume that there was a railway worker involved in the gang, they could quite easily have been riding in the baggage car. After all, it is next to the coach we were in, and all they had to do was drug us with the chloroform and then take the money back into the baggage car again. If they did that, we would never find it, no matter how many times we searched the passenger cars."

3

"Surely, the fact that they managed to hijack a whole train would indicate that the gang included at least one member who worked for the railway, and if that was so, it would not be impossible for him to arrange for someone to ride in the baggage coach." Honda continued, "Once they had moved the money in there, it would be easy for them to get it off the train. No passengers left the train during the service stops, but the conductor said that some freight was unloaded and they could simply have unloaded the money at the same time."

He had been keeping his voice down as he spoke because he did not want to offend Kitano, who, after all, was also employed by the railway, but his voice rose as he warmed to his theme and Kitano must have overheard him because he said, "I don't want to think that any member of our organization was involved in this case."

Totsugawa nodded.

"I realize how you feel, but you must admit that there is a lot to Honda's theory. The baggage car is next to the car that carried the money, and it is also the one place that we did not search."

"I still think you are wrong."

"Why?" Honda asked.

"Because the baggage car is locked on both sides and only the chief conductor has the key to open the door from this side. Personally, I don't think he is a member of the gang."

"I certainly agree with you there," Totsugawa said.

Honda agreed, nodding, but added, "In that case, what has happened to the money?"

The train pulled into Ichinohe and then pulled out again almost immediately. It only stopped there and at the next station, Sannohe, for thirty seconds as only a few people used either of these stations. At eight thirty-four the train pulled into Hachinohe for a two-minute stop. Hachinohe is a large fishing and industrial city and it was there that the five men who had cleared away the berths left the train. Twenty-nine of the passengers also got off, and none of them had the money with them when they did.

The next station was Misawa, and at this rate, they would arrive there no wiser as to how the kidnappers managed to spirit the money away.

"You don't think those five men were suspicious, do you?" Totsugawa suddenly asked as the train had started to move. He could still see them walking down the platform, but they soon disappeared as the train picked up speed.

"But they weren't carrying anything."

"Yes, I know that, but when they folded the berths away they had the passengers move out into the corridor and although the bottom berth becomes the seat and it would be impossible to hide anything there, the upper berth folds away into the ceiling and surely that would be an ideal place to hide the money?"

4

"You mean you think they hid the money and then got off the train at Hachinohe?" Honda asked.

The train was accelerating on its way to Misawa, and the hot morning sun streamed in through the open curtains.

"Yes, each member of the gang may have their own special job and theirs was just to hide the money. This train is going to be left in the sidings at Aomori for a while, isn't it?"

"Yes, it will go to the yard for an overhaul," said Kitano.

Totsugawa nodded.

"That would mean they could have someone waiting there and he could pick up the money later on."

"You seem to forget, Totsugawa, we were with them the whole time they were working. There were two policemen with each worker, watching their every move in case the money should come to light, so I think it very unlikely that they would have the chance to hide anything," Honda said.

"I agree with Mr. Honda," Kitano said. "I think it would be quite impossible for them to do something like that without one of us noticing."

"But in that case, what has happened to the money?" Totsugawa asked, looking around the carriage.

Now that the bunks had been folded away, it was no different from any other express train, and the passengers could be seen sitting opposite each other, chatting happily. For a moment it looked so peaceful that Totsugawa could almost believe that all of them were part of the plot. One billion yen divided up among three hundred people would leave them with three million each. A small sum like that would be easy to hide. He knew that this could not really be the case, however; it would hardly be worth their while kidnapping a whole train full of passengers for such a small sum. Also, it would be virtually impossible for them to book all the seats on the train, and if there were some passengers on board who were not connected with the gang, they would probably notice when the others started to split up the money.

"You know, I think the money must already have been taken off the train," he said bleakly.

This would mean that they had been beaten by the kidnappers. Not only had they failed to arrest them, but they had also let them get away with the money and they still did not have even the slightest idea who they were. He did not want to believe that the kidnappers had got away with the money; he wanted to think that they were still on the train, waiting for a chance to get off somewhere. But they had looked every possible place now, and it seemed impossible that the money could still be on the train.

"But how do you think they managed to get the money off?" Kitano asked.

"I can only suppose that they managed to get it off the train soon after leaving Mito, while we were all unconscious. If that is so, it means that we have been wasting our time having the railway police help us search the passengers' luggage."

"When you came to the train was moving, wasn't it?"

"Yes, it was traveling at about forty miles per hour, but the money had disappeared."

"But we were told that when the train stopped at Taira Station, the doors weren't opened and nobody got off. If that was the case, surely it would be impossible to get the money off the train?"

"I thought so too, but we have searched the train from end to end without finding anything. That can only mean the money was already off the train when we came to. Although nobody left the train, I think they must have managed to get the sacks of money off somehow. They probably had an accomplice waiting at a prearranged spot. He would have been able to pick it up without anyone seeing them as it was the middle of the night."

"But how could they get the money off the train?" Kitano asked, his tone making it plain that he thought it impossible.

"I have been wondering the same thing," Totsugawa said, looking around the interior of the car again.

Could they have switched one of the doors to manual and used that to throw the money out while the train was still running? But no, the only person who could switch the doors from automatic to manual was the chief conductor, and he was above suspicion. The windows were all sealed except for the one in the washroom and that was too small . . .

"Let's take a walk and see," he said.

5

Totsugawa walked from car number one to number two. Honda went with him, but neither of them could see anywhere that could have been used to throw the money off the train. They continued through cars two, three, and four, but it was just the same. Suddenly, as they were about to go through to car number five, Totsugawa stopped, and Honda, who was taking up the rear, almost bumped into him.

"What is it?"

"What's under this plate?" he asked, squatting down and peering at the steel plate that linked the corridors of the two coaches. The train was moving at high speed and the plate was swaying around quite violently.

"I think it covers the coupling between this and the next coach."

Totsugawa grabbed the heavy metal plate and lifted it. Underneath was not the coupling, but a heavy, imitation-leather bellows that was bolted to both cars to prevent any passengers from injuring themselves if they fell.

"What if you cut this?" he asked, looking up at Honda.

Honda leaned forward to see and Totsugawa tapped it with his finger.

"If they had cut a hole in the side, we would soon realize what had happened, but if they did it under this plate, we would never know."

"You think they threw the money out of here?"

"Yes, they could have thrown the bags out one after the

other and had an accomplice standing by to retrieve them from
the tracks. That way they would only need one or two men on the
train."

"Where do you think they cut the hole?"

"Oh, I think it is pretty certain to have been between cars
one and two, where everyone had been drugged by the chloroform. The whole of car one had been booked by a single group,
so once the conductor had checked the tickets, there would be no
reason for him to go back there again. Also, being at the very end
of the train, there was very little likelihood of anyone passing
through, so they needn't worry about being seen while they were
at work."

They hurried back to the entrance to car number one and
lifted up the steel plate. They looked down and, sure enough,
they could see the track rushing by through a rectangular hole
that had been cut in one side of the bellows. Totsugawa reached
down and stretched the hole until it was about ten inches across.
It was obvious that this was where the money had been thrown off
the train.

"Damn it!" Honda exclaimed, although it was very rare for
him to raise his voice in such a manner.

"Well, at least we now know why they stipulated that the
bags should be ten inches wide, any bigger and they would not
have fitted through the hole."

"Also the length was not only to do with the size of the
bunks. There is less than a yard to spare between here and the
track; if they were any longer, they might not fall through
properly."

"That means that the money . . ." he gritted his teeth in
vexation.

Totsugawa put the plate back into position.

"They probably did this soon after they knocked us out with
the chloroform. They probably had timed the train the day before
so they would know where it would be at a certain time and
arranged for one of their accomplices to be waiting in his car by

the tracks. At the prearranged time, all they had to do was throw the sacks out through the hole and then go back to their berths as if nothing had happened. After that, they only had to wait until the train stopped at Ichinoseki or somewhere and then get off as if they were just ordinary passengers."

"Damn!" said Honda again.

They showed the hole to Kitano who gave a deep sigh.

"So this means that we have lost our chance of catching the kidnappers after all; our only chance had been to get them when they picked up the ransom."

"I don't agree," Totsugawa said, already recovering from his disappointment.

"But we handed over one billion yen in ransom without getting so much as a glance at the kidnapper's face."

"That is true."

"Also, there is very little chance that anyone saw them when they picked up the money from the tracks. This was the last train of the day; all the railway staff would already have gone home and there would be nobody around to see them. They certainly chose a good train for their plan: they would be able to pick up the money at their leisure without having to worry about being seen."

"But there are still the hostages."

"Do you think the kidnappers will let them go unharmed?"

THE PURSUIT

1

Now that they knew the kidnappers had managed to get away with the money, there was no need for Kitano, Honda, and Totsugawa to remain on the train. They all wanted to get back to Tokyo as soon as possible in order to plan their next move.

Kitano telephoned Kimoto from Misawa and then all three boarded a Towa airlines DC-9 for Tokyo. They arrived at Tokyo's Haneda Airport at ten-fifty, and by the time they arrived at J.N.R.'s head office it was already eleven-forty. The Mystery Train was supposed to have returned to Tokyo Station at nine-thirty that morning and they all wondered what had happened. Either the kidnappers had kept their promise and returned both the train and its passengers, or Tokyo Station would be flooded with calls from the relatives of the missing people.

They walked into the director's office, but he did not make any comment about the fact that they had lost the money and had failed to catch the kidnappers.

"Welcome back," he said.

"I am very sorry," Honda said and bowed deeply.

Kitano looked at the clock.

"Has the Mystery Train returned?" This was the question that was foremost in all their minds.

Kimoto blinked his bloodshot eyes and looked up at them.

"I had a call from the kidnapper again just after you called. It was at nine-thirty, the time that the train was due to have arrived in Tokyo."

"What did he say?"

"I recorded the call so I think it would be quicker if you just listened to it yourselves."

He pressed a button on the tape recorder and they heard the same, familiar voice.

"*Is that Kimoto?*"

"*Yes, you have got your money so I want you to release the hostages straight away—the train, too.*"

"*It is true that I got the money, but I have decided to hold on to the hostages for another twenty-four hours.*"

"*Why? This isn't what we agreed. You promised you would release the train and the hostages as soon as you received the money.*"

"*Yes, but I only got nine hundred million. You were one hundred million short.*"

"*Don't be ridiculous, we did everything just as you wanted. We put one billion yen in ten sacks and put them on the night express to Aomori. You or your accomplice took the money and dropped it off the train by cutting the cover between the carriages. We kept our end of the bargain.*"

"*That is true, but no matter how hard we looked, we could only find nine bags, that means that we are one hundred million short, so we cannot let you have the hostages back.*"

"*Are you sure that one of your men is not pulling a fast one on you? Then again, are you just saying this in an effort to get more money out of us?*"

"*I am just stating a fact. We asked for one billion yen but all we got was nine hundred million. I will hold on to the hostages for*

*another twenty-four hours and during that time I want you to get
the last hundred million."*

"I keep telling you, we have already paid one billion."

*"Okay, I'll tell you what, I will let you have the train back.
We have got nine hundred million, after all, and that rolling stock
is valuable property to J.N.R."*

"But what about the passengers?"

2

The tape ended with the sound of the kidnapper breaking
the connection.

"He's lying!" Kitano exclaimed angrily. "All ten bags disappeared so how can he claim that he was one hundred million
short?"

"Did you have the track checked between Mito and Taira?"
Totsugawa asked quietly.

"Yes, as soon as I heard from you what happened I had the
track maintenance teams check the whole track, but they did not
come up with anything. The kidnappers must have collected all
the bags while it was still dark."

"In that case it is a bit strange that he should phone and say
that he was one hundred million short."

"That is why I say he is lying. Once he actually got his hands
on the money, he became greedy and decided to try for more."

"Maybe we should not take his talk of returning the rolling
stock seriously either," Kimoto said.

"From what we know of him, I would say that we cannot
trust him at all. He does not seem to be the type who bothers very
much about keeping his promises. But if he does not return the
train and passengers, what are we going to do? We will be
inundated with inquiries from the passengers' relatives," Kitano
said, voicing his main concern.

"Yes, I was very worried about that, too, so I sent the chief of the passenger section, Shibata, over to Tokyo Station to try and sort things out. He should be coming back shortly."

Kitano allowed himself to relax. If anyone could sort out this mess, it would be Shibata. He was an expert on the railways, and although he may not be the smartest man in the organization, he was totally devoted to it and could be relied on to do his utmost.

It was about fifteen minutes later when Shibata hurried into the director's office. He was a small, plump man and there was a sheen of perspiration on his forehead when he hurried in. He nodded vaguely toward Kitano and the two detectives and then made his report to Kimoto.

"I think I have been able to put them off for a while."

"What did you do?"

"There were about fifty people at the station to meet the train and we had another twenty telephone calls asking why the train had been delayed, among them was one from the wife of the famous actor, Ko Nishimoto. His ten-year-old son is on the train, you know."

"And what did you say to them?"

"Well, I thought if I told them that the train had been delayed, they would want to know what time it would be due in, so, first of all, I explained the planned route. First the visit to the steam museum at Umekoji, then a visit to the sand dunes at Tottori, and then down to Okayama and home via the Sanyo and Tokaido lines."

"Then what?"

"I said that when they were visiting the steam museum at Umekoji, a lot of people said that they wanted to go to Yamaguchi Prefecture and see the steam engines that are still running there. This idea spread in popularity until the Osaka office felt obliged to agree and the Mystery Train was diverted from Tottori to run down the coast to Masuda and from there to the Yamaguchi line where they could see the steam locomotives. After that, it was to go down to Ogori and then back to Tokyo, but as a result of this change in plan, the trip would take twenty-four hours longer than had been originally announced and it would not return until tomorrow morning. I also left instructions that any further inquiries should be met with the same explanation."

"I see, and did they believe you?"

"I think so. A lot of them were parents of the children on the train and they had probably been pestered to go to see the steam engines countless times before, so they had no reason to doubt me."

"How about the press?"

"They don't seem to have realized anything yet, there have been so many special trains like the Mystery Train recently that it does not have much news value. I know it is a terrible thing to say, but we were lucky that the plane accident took the heat off us."

"Plane accident?"

"Yes, haven't you heard?"

"No, I have been so taken up by the Mystery Train that I have not seen the papers or the television."

"It was too late for the regular morning papers so they brought out a special edition. I've got a copy here."

So saying he took a newspaper out of his pocket and spread it on the table.

THIRTY CASUALTIES IN CRASH LANDING!
A.N.A. AIRLINES BOEING 747SR FROM TOKYO CRASHES ON LANDING AT NAHA AIRPORT, OKINAWA.

3

The newspaper did not carry any details.

"The press and TV are busy trying to find out the details of this crash," Shibata said.

"Yes, but if they found out that four hundred people were being held hostage, they would soon be after us."

"Yes, I agree, and unfortunately there is someone who knows that the train never reached Tottori."

"You mean someone from the outside?"

"Worse than that, a reporter who works for a magazine called *Ryoso*. Her name is Yukiko Norikane."

"Yes, I know that magazine. They recently interviewed me about the future of J.N.R. But how did she find out the train was missing?"

"A colleague of hers was on the Mystery Train to report on the trip and he had promised to call her yesterday. However, she did not hear anything from him, so she came to Tokyo Station to find out what had happened to the train and met assistant stationmaster Aoki who she knew from a story she had done in the past. He had no idea that anything had happened to the train and when he telephoned Tottori for her he found out that the train was missing."

"I see, but she does not know the details about the hijack?"

"No, of course not."

"When does that magazine come out?"

"The twenty-fifth."

"We still have fifteen days then, so I don't think we need worry. We had better keep our eye on her though."

As he spoke, the phone on his desk rang and everyone in the room tensed. Honda nodded and Kitano answered it but soon offered the receiver to Totsugawa.

"It is for you, from a Detective Kamei."

Totsugawa took the phone.

"Hello, Kamei? What do you want?"

"We have found a body in Tama River that I think may be connected with your case."

"A body?" he repeated and looked over to Honda.

"Okay, you get over there," Honda said. "I can handle this end on my own. I want you to stick with this case; you can use as many people as you think is necessary, just don't forget to keep in touch."

This was a relief for Totsugawa. As things stood, all they could do was wait for the kidnapper to contact them again, but now he could be out doing something positive. He headed straight for the police headquarters near the emperor's palace and found Kamei waiting for him.

"Fill me in," he said.

"Well, yesterday the naked body of a man was found by the bank of Tama River near the Rokugo bridge. It was estimated that the dead man was about thirty-five or -six."

"Rokugo bridge, that means it falls under the jurisdiction of the West Kamata station, doesn't it?"

"Yes. At first it was thought that the man had been unable to stand the heat and gone for a swim in the nude, and when he got into the water the cold caused him to have a heart attack."

"And that was wrong?"

"Yes, the body was autopsied and it would appear that he was strangled. There were a number of bruises of the body, too."

"Murder?"

"Yes, an investigation headquarters was set up at Kamata an hour ago."

"But what has this to do with the Mystery Train investigation?"

Kamei leaned forward.

"Well, although we still don't know the identity of the dead man, our people at Kamata told me that he had a line on his forehead that would seem to indicate that the dead man wore a hat."

"But nobody wears hats these days."

"Nobody, that is, except for those people who have to wear a uniform like policemen, soldiers, firemen, and . . ."

"Railway men."

"Exactly, railway conductors wear caps, and according to the autopsy the man in question died between ten and twelve on the night of August the eighth."

"I see, the Mystery Train was supposed to leave at one

minute to midnight on the eighth but it was delayed for about six minutes because the conductor was late."

"Do you think it would be worth checking up on this body?"

"Of course, what are we waiting for?"

4

When they arrived at West Kamata police station they went straight down to the morgue and looked at the body, which had been returned from the hospital where the autopsy was done.

The dead man had been about five feet seven inches tall and well built. As they had heard in the report, his suntan stopped halfway up his forehead, making it obvious that he wore a hat. He was completely nude and there was not so much as a ring or watch on the body.

A young detective named Hasegawa filled them in on the details.

"We have searched both banks of the river but we have not been able to find any of the dead man's possessions. Of course, they may have been washed away by the river, but we feel it is more likely that they were taken by his assailant."

"Who found the body?"

"Some children who were playing nearby."

They had the young detective point out on a map where the body had been found and then they went to check the spot for themselves. There were still plenty of children playing and fishing in the vicinity, and there were also a number of couples moving about on the river in boats. The sun glittered off the water and the whole scene was very peaceful until a train crossed the nearby bridge with a loud roar.

"Is that Rokugo bridge?" Totsugawa asked, watching the train as it disappeared.

"Yes, the Tokaido line crosses the river there."

"Yes, it is the same one that the Mystery Train used after it left Tokyo," Totsugawa said, visualizing a map in his mind. The train left Tokyo, passed through Shinagawa, and crossed this bridge. The next station was Kawasaki, but the night train went on to the station after that, Yokohama, before it stopped. The train would have crossed this bridge twenty minutes after leaving Tokyo Station, but had the body been thrown from the train or had it been brought here by car and dumped in the river?

"Why do you think the body was stripped before it was dumped?" Totsugawa asked Kamei as they walked along the river.

"I should think it was done to hide the man's identity. We still have no idea who he might be and although we guessed that he might be a conductor, it is pure supposition; we still have no real proof."

"But surely if the murderer really wanted to hide the man's identity he would have disfigured the face, but there isn't a mark on it aside from its being slightly bloated due to the strangulation."

"Maybe the murderer was confident that we would not be able to trace his identity straight away even without going to those lengths. There is that body of a young woman that we found in a hotel in Shinjuku three months ago. She had not been disfigured either, but the murderer took away all her belongings and we still have not been able to trace her identity."

"That's a point. He may not be from Tokyo, not from this area anyway, so the murderer felt quite sure that we would not quickly find out his identity."

"What shall we do now?"

"I take it that his fingerprints have been checked."

"Yes, but whoever he was, he did not have a record."

"If he worked for the railway it seems very likely that he was connected with the Mystery Train. Why don't we just investigate that side of it and leave the rest to the local boys?"

"Shall we take a picture of his face and show it to the people at Tokyo Station?"

"Yes, that would be the quickest way. If he really is a conductor, it makes the whole case much more interesting."

5

A photograph of a dead man's face often bears little resemblance to the way the man had looked in life, especially in a case of strangulation where the face tends to be rather bloated, so Totsugawa had an artist come in and make a drawing. He drew three pictures, one of the corpse's face as it was, one with the swelling removed and a slight smile on the face, and finally one that Totsugawa had requested especially: the same as the second one but wearing a conductor's cap.

They took the three pictures to the conductor's office in Tokyo Station. This is situated on the second floor of the red-brick station building and is used by over three hundred conductors.

Totsugawa met with the supervisor and said, "I believe this man is a conductor and I wondered if you recognized him."

The supervisor took the pictures and looked at them for some time but did not come to a decision. While he was still trying to make up his mind, some conductors who had just clocked in walked by on their way to work, each with a large case in his hand.

"I am sorry, he is not one of ours," the supervisor said finally.

"Could he belong to another branch?"

"Are you sure that he is a conductor?"

"I think so," Totsugawa answered noncommittally.

At that moment one of the conductors looked over to see what was going on and when he saw the picture, he said, "What has he done?"

"Do you know this man?" the supervisor asked in surprise.

"Yes, his name is Uehara, he works for the Osaka office."

"Are you quite sure?" Totsugawa asked.

"Yes, last year I shared a room with him at Hakone on the Union trip. There is no doubt about it, that's Uehara, but why do you want to know? What has he done?"

"It was the Osaka office that organized the Mystery Train, wasn't it?"

"That is correct," replied the supervisor.

"The train left from Tokyo Station, but would it have been possible for an Osaka conductor to be on board?"

"Of course, they were all from Osaka. It was an Osaka train."

"You have not heard of any conductors suddenly disappearing some time around the eighth of this month, have you?"

"No, I haven't heard any rumors like that."

"Can you get in touch with the Osaka office from here?"

"Yes, of course."

"Well, in that case, do you think you could find out what train Uehara is supposed to be on at the moment and also something about his background?"

"Certainly, just a moment please."

The supervisor went over to his desk to make the call. He spoke for about ten minutes, making notes while he did so.

"Yes, well, his full name is Kyuji Uehara, age thirty-two, and at the moment he is supposed to be on board the Mystery Train."

"Just as I thought."

This was a big step forward. Until now, they knew absolutely nothing about the Mystery Train since it had disappeared. Now, for the first time, they had a lead even though Uehara was dead and could not tell them anything.

"He has worked for the railway for eleven years and he lives with his wife and child in the Tenoji area of Osaka. His hobby is mah-jongg and he likes to drink. Is that all you need to know?" the supervisor asked, looking up from his memo.

6

The Osaka sales manager, Kusaka, looked very grim as he talked to his chief administrator. Kusaka had been the one who first thought up the idea for the Mystery Train and was considered to be one of the most promising men in the office. He had planned many similar attractions in the past, but because of the Mystery Train's popularity, its disappearance had been a disaster for him. In Japan, a man's forty-second year is said to be very unlucky, and he wondered briefly if this was why it had happened to him. Despite that, however, he found it impossible to believe a whole train could just disappear like that, and he was determined to get to the bottom of it.

"I intend to look for the Mystery Train and find out what happened to it," he said.

"What do you mean look for it? Where do you intend to start?" Asai, the administrator, looked almost as cross as he had when he took on the trade unions the year before.

"Well, we know that the passengers on the Mystery Train all went to visit the steam museum at Umekoji on the ninth. I thought if I was to go there and ask around, I might be able to come up with some clue as to where they went after that."

"Well, I hope you do. If we cannot find that train I am afraid that I will have to take the responsibility." He wished him luck and then Kusaka left the office.

It was still as hot as ever, and while Kusaka liked hot weather, the last three days had been too much even for him. He told himself that once this mess with the Mystery Train had been sorted out, he would treat himself to a holiday in Hokkaido where it would be a little cooler.

He took one of the new limited express trains to Kyoto, a trip of about thirty minutes, and went to the steam museum by taxi. He got out of the taxi and, going through a small tunnel, found himself at the entrance. Admission was two hundred yen with a discount for parties. Back in the days when steam locomotives had been the craze among schoolchildren, the museum had been filled to overflowing every day; now it was not nearly so popular.

Despite the fact that he worked for J.N.R., this was the first time he had visited the museum, and he looked around with interest. In the middle there was a large turntable and behind that there was a large engine shed that held several huge, black locomotives. Being the summer holidays, it was quite crowded with children, sitting on the hard concrete, drawing the trains, and chatting loudly.

Kusaka found one of the employees and asked him some questions. Like most of the people who worked there he was an old man—this was one of the places where railway men go for employment after retirement.

"There should have been a large group of visitors here yesterday morning who came on the Mystery Train, do you remember them?"

The man he had found was a small old man with a heavy suntan and deeply lined face. Kusaka guessed that he had probably been an engine driver somewhere when he was young.

"Yes, they arrived at about ten o'clock and stayed for about an hour."

"You are quite sure that they were from the Mystery Train?"

"Yes, the man who was leading the group told me so himself. It was a Sunday and there were a lot of other visitors, so the place was quite crowded again for a change."

From the way he spoke, it was obvious that he preferred it when the museum was crowded.

"They were supposed to have come by bus . . ."

"Yes, that is correct. There were a whole lot of buses lined up outside."

According to his plan, the Mystery Train was supposed to pull into platform six at Kyoto Station where the electric locomotive would be changed for a diesel. While this was going on, the passengers were to board a fleet of large buses and spend an hour looking at the steam trains at Umekoji.

Well, so far so good, he thought. At least he now knew for sure that the passengers had come this far, but where did they go after that? He guessed that they went back to the Mystery Train, but he had no idea what could have happened afterward since they never appeared at Tottori, the next stop.

Kusaka went back to his taxi, which he had had wait for him, and told the driver to take him back to Kyoto Station.

Inside, he looked for the assistant stationmaster, who took him to platform six.

"Do you remember the Mystery Train? It arrived here at about nine-thirty yesterday morning and the locomotive was changed from electric to diesel."

"Sure, I remember the Mystery Train. I waited here on the platform for it myself. We were told that there would be four hundred passengers arriving, so we arranged for Miss Kyoto to be here to greet them with a bouquet of flowers, but the train never appeared. Next time when you change your plans like that, I would appreciate it if you could tell us."

At first Kusaka thought the other man was joking, but then he saw that he was quite serious.

"But that can't be . . ." he exclaimed in disbelief.

ANOTHER
MURDER

1

Kusaka could not understand it, the assistant stationmaster said that he had waited on this platform for the Mystery Train but it had never arrived. However, one of the attendants at Umekoji had just told him that the train's passengers had been at the museum on schedule. That was why it had been assumed that the train had arrived safely.

"Let me ask you one more time. Are you quite sure that at nine-thirty on the morning of the ninth, the Mystery Train failed to arrive at this platform?"

"Yes, absolutely. I waited here for thirty minutes; when it failed to show up I assumed that the schedule must have been changed and told Miss Kyoto that she could go home."

"Why didn't you contact us at the Osaka office and tell us that the train hadn't arrived?"

The stationmaster looked annoyed.

"I hate to have to say this, but your Mystery Train was only a special train and it is all we can do to keep the regular trains running on schedule. I don't know about Tokyo or Osaka, but Kyoto is a world-famous tourist center and Sunday is the busiest

71

day of the week for us. Yesterday we had all kinds of visitors from overseas, and it is my job as assistant stationmaster to look after them. I had to entertain a delegation from Rome Station and it is also my job to negotiate with the union. Would you like me to show you my schedule for that day?"

"No, that is quite all right," Kusaka said hurriedly, realizing that he might not be altogether popular with the station workers, but the stationmaster was not finished with him yet.

"Another thing, when the Mystery Train failed to show up, you contacted Umekoji and asked them whether the passengers had been there, but you never thought of checking with us as to whether the train had arrived or not. This is the first time anyone has bothered to ask me about it."

"Yes, I'm sorry, but when we heard that the passengers had arrived at the steam museum, we just automatically assumed that the train had reached here safely," Kusaka said with a shrug.

"Yes, but don't you think you have got your priorities wrong?"

"What do you mean?"

"Well, you think up all these special trains and all you worry about are the attractions on the route, the visit to the steam museum or the trip to the sand dunes at Tottori. But I am afraid that we are much more interested in just ensuring that the regular trains all run safely and according to schedule. On the ninth, your Mystery Train did not arrive here, but we did not hear any reports of an accident and all the other trains were running on time, so we were quite happy. As far as we are concerned, that is all that matters."

"Okay, okay, I understand."

2

Kusaka left Kyoto Station. He was well known as an idea man and he had appeared several times in magazines as being representative of the new breed of railwayman, but now that the Mystery Train had disappeared, he was beginning to discover that he was not as popular among the average railwaymen as he would like to have thought. The main reason was that although his ideas may have been popular with his superiors, they just meant more work for the people who worked in the stations.

Be that as it may, he still had to find the four hundred missing passengers, or, as his boss had said, the Osaka office would be made to take the blame.

The square in front of the station was filled with tourists. In particular, there was a large number of young people waiting for buses to take them to Sagano and outlying areas. It must have been very similar to this the previous morning, except that there would have been a number of coaches waiting to take the passengers from the Mystery Train to the steam museum. In Tottori it had been arranged for buses owned by J.N.R. to take the passengers to the sand dunes, but here there had not been enough to spare, so they were chartered from a private operator. Kusaka decided to go to the Kyonan Bus Company, which had handled the job, and see what light they could throw on the mystery. He crossed the square and walked into the company's main office, which was situated opposite the station.

"Yes, we transported the passengers of the Mystery Train from here to the steam museum at Umekoji," said the branch manager, Kinoshita, as he leafed through a pile of papers.

"Could you tell me about it in detail, please?" Kusaka asked, looking around the office. The walls were covered with posters advertising day tours of the city and special tours of the temples.

"There is not really very much to tell. We just took the passengers to the museum as requested. We were told that there would be four hundred people, which meant that we would need ten forty-seat coaches, but it being a Sunday and the summer holidays and all, we could only manage to get five.

"Umekoji is not very far away and we thought that we could ferry the passengers there in two trips. I had the buses wait in the street outside here, but in the end, we managed to take them all in one trip."

"Why is that?"

"Only about two hundred people turned up, so we managed to fit them all into the five coaches that we had."

"That is odd; there were supposed to be four hundred passengers on the train."

"Yes, I thought so, too, and I asked your tour leader about it, but he told me that half of the passengers were still tired after their night on the train, and that they had decided to stay on the train and rest. We run a lot of trips for school outings, you know, and it is the same on them, half the students sleep through the trip," Kinoshita said with a laugh.

"Where did the group come from?" Kusaka asked, and Kinoshita gave him a strange look.

"Why, they walked over from the station, of course."

"You said that you spoke to the tour leader."

"Yes . . ."

"Could you describe him to me?"

"He was a quiet man in his forties. He knew a lot about the railways and told us all kinds of interesting stories."

"For instance?"

"Why are you asking me all this? Has something happened?"

"No, I just want to know for future reference."

"I see. Well, he told us that they were making feasibility studies on running the bullet train at night and all about various special trains they have planned in the past."

"Did he sign any documents for you?"

"Yes, after we brought them back to the station, he signed this for me."

Kinoshita pulled out a sheet of paper from the pile he was sorting and showed it to Kusaka.

The signature at the bottom said Okabe, which was correct, as the leader of the tour was in fact the Osaka sales manager,

Yoshio Okabe. The description fit him, too. He was about forty
and he had been chosen to lead the tour because of his quiet
personality. However, was the signature on the bottom of the
document really Okabe's?

"What did this Okabe look like?"

"Let me see, he had rather a round face and was wearing
glasses."

"What was he wearing, an ordinary suit?"

"No, he was wearing a kind of white suit. I think it was a
railway uniform. I remember thinking that he must have been
very hot, wearing a tie like that in this weather."

Kinoshita was wearing a tie himself.

The description of a round-faced man wearing glasses would
certainly fit Okabe, and a white suite was one of the uniforms
used by the railway, but if it had really been Okabe, why hadn't
he reported when the train had failed to arrive in Kyoto Station?

"May I borrow this document for two or three days please?"
he asked, indicating the paper that Okabe had signed.

3

At about the same time Kinoshita was talking with the bus
company official, Kitano had received an interesting report.
Apparently, someone living near Nakoso Station on the Joban
line had found thirty ten-thousand yen notes near the railway,
and several scraps of canvas similar to that used in the money
bags had been discovered on the tracks there.

"Well, now we know why the kidnapper complained that he
was one hundred million short," he remarked to Kimoto.

"You mean that the bag broke and the money blew away?"

"Yes, I think it is quite likely that that is what happened.
They dropped the money off the train at the couplings where
there are all kinds of pipes and connections on which the bags
could have been caught. If one had been ripped open, the wind

from the train's passage would blow the money over a wide area. I think the money found was part of the ransom."

"You mean that one hundred million just blew away?"

"I'm afraid so. I have asked the police to collect as much as possible, but I doubt that they will be able to find it all."

"I hope the kidnappers will believe that that is what happened."

Honda came back from the next room where he had been talking to Totsugawa on the phone.

"It would appear that a conductor from the Osaka office has been murdered," he told Kimoto.

"Was he one of the men on the Mystery Train?"

"Yes. He was found naked in Tama River near Rokugo bridge."

"Is his death connected to the train's disappearance?"

"We don't know yet, although it would appear that he died before the train was due to leave Tokyo Station."

"So you don't know why he was killed?"

"Not yet, but I think that when we know the answer to that, we will know what his connection is with the present case. We still have one other lead that we want to check on, though. Last night the kidnapper told us to put the money on bunk sixteen in the last car of the night express. The whole of that car had been booked by a tour group, and it is strange that the only member who failed to turn up was the man who was supposed to use that bunk, a Mr. Ishiyama. Of course, this could have been a coincidence, but I don't think so. Our man is not one to leave things like that to chance. I have told Totsugawa to find out as much about this Ishiyama as he can."

"Well, I hope he comes up with some kind of a clue."

At that moment the phone rang and Kimoto looked at his watch. It was exactly two P.M.

It is him again, Honda thought.

Kimoto picked up the phone and the tape started to turn. It was the kidnapper.

"Have you got the money ready?"

"I want to talk to you about that. Apparently one of the bags burst when you threw it off the train and the money was scattered down the tracks. Someone who lives nearby found some of the money. I am sure that it will be on the news if you look," Kimoto said, doing his best to convince the man.

"I find that a little hard to believe."

"But it's true, watch the TV news if you don't believe me. We kept our side of the bargain and paid the full amount, so you should keep yours and give us back the hostages straight away."

"Even if it is true, it does not change anything."

"What are you talking about?"

"When I get the final hundred million I will let the hostages go. I will give you one more hour to get the money ready. Think of it, you will be able to save four hundred people for a mere hundred million."

4

The travel club, Nennikai, had started in the letters column of the magazine *Traveler* and was organized by a doctor named Ota who lived in the Yotsuya area of Tokyo. The club itself was on a four-day trip to the Shimokita peninsula, but Dr. Ota had been unable to accompany the others. Totsugawa and Kamei went to visit him and when they rang the door chimes they were greeted by a man in his fifties with a crutch.

"I am afraid I fell down in the mountains and broke my leg," he said, laughing self-consciously. "The Nennikai was started by a group of readers of a travel magazine who wanted the opportunity to go on trips around the country twice a year—in fact the name means 'twice a year.'"

"Do you have the names and addresses of all the members here?"

"Yes, of course, but they are all good people. I do not think any of them would do anything that would involve them with the police."

Ota shook his head disbelievingly and Totsugawa hurried to reassure him.

"We are only looking for a member who seems to have gone missing."

"What is his name?"

"Ishiyama, he works for the Taiyo Manufacturing Company."

"Oh, I know Mr. Ishiyama very well; he should be on the trip to Mount Osore at the moment."

"Yes, I know, but he did not catch the train with the others last night. We waited until the train left the station, but he still did not appear."

"That is very unlike him. He always takes part in our trips and never lets us down."

"Could you let us have his telephone number?"

"Certainly."

Ota took out a list of the members and gave them Ishiyama's home and work numbers. Since it was still afternoon, Totsugawa called the work number first but was told that Ishiyama had taken a holiday and would not be back until Tuesday the eleventh. It would appear that he had intended to go on the trip after all—or he was a member of the gang of kidnappers and that was why his berth was chosen to leave the money. He tried the home number, but there was no answer.

"Is Mr. Ishiyama married?"

Ota thought for a few moments.

"No, he is still a bachelor I think. When we went on our trip to Kyushu last April, I remember him mentioning that he wanted to get married soon."

"Did he ever mention that he was hard up for money?"

"No, never. His parents run a large hotel at Kusatsu, so I think it unlikely that he would ever be in need of money. Actually, our group plans to stay at his hotel next winter."

"Who organized the trip to the Shimokita peninsula?"

"Well, as I mentioned earlier, our group likes to go on a trip twice a year and once we have decided on a destination, a member who comes from that area or one who has been there for a holiday before takes it upon himself to organize it. This time the trip was planned by someone who originally comes from Aomori, a man named Kojima. He is an illustrator."

They copied down Kojima's address and telephone number, too, and then left.

5

Seiji Ishiyama lived in a ten-story condominium about eight minutes' walk from Nakano Station. Totsugawa and Kamei walked in and, after checking the mailboxes for the apartment number, found that the one they wanted was on the seventh floor. They went up in the elevator and looked for the room. Most of the apartments seemed to belong to working people as the whole building was very quiet and there was no sign of life. They soon found the door they were looking for and rang the bell. There was no answer and the door was locked, so Kamei bent down to look through the keyhole. When he did he was assailed by a putrid smell. He recognized it immediately as being that of a rotting body and hurried down to get the caretaker to open the door for them.

The apartment consisted of two rooms and a kitchen, and in one of the rooms facing on to the balcony they found the body of a man dressed in pajamas and lying face down. All the windows in the room were closed and with the curtains drawn it was unbearably hot. In temperatures like this, it would not take long for a body to start to smell.

Kamei put a handkerchief over his nose to try and hold back the smell. He turned the body over.

"Is this Mr. Ishiyama?" he asked.

The caretaker, a man in his early forties and wearing a beige uniform, looked as if he was about to faint, but he managed to nod.

It was obviously a murder. The body had the wire from a light stand wrapped around its neck and there was some dried blood on the back of the head. It would appear that the murderer had struck him from behind and then used the wire to finish him off.

They called for an investigation team, which soon arrived together with a coroner who Totsugawa knew named Sanada. He was a good man but was rather lacking in delicacy.

"What a stink!" he said as he started to examine the body.

"When do you think he was killed?" Totsugawa asked.

"A day has passed since he died, I would say some time yesterday afternoon."

"Can't you give me a more precise time?"

"That's impossible; I am not God, you know. I might be able to tell you a bit more after I have completed my autopsy."

If he had been killed on the ninth, it meant he died the day after the Mystery Train had disappeared, or rather the day that the ransom money was paid. After the investigation team had finished taking its photos and completed checking for fingerprints and the body had been removed, Totsugawa opened the window wide to let the smell out of the room.

"Why do you think he was killed?" Kamei asked.

"That is the question. Was he a member of the gang from the beginning, or did the kidnapper just ask him if they could use his berth to collect the ransom and when he refused murdered him? If we knew the answer to that, it would be a great help in finding out who his murderer was."

"So you think his murder is connected with the disappearance of the Mystery Train?"

"Yes, the room has not been disturbed and the corpse was wearing a gold pendant. Gold is one of the easiest things to dispose of, so if it was a robber who killed him, he would never have left that behind."

"If he was a member of the gang, it would certainly make things much easier for us."

Totsugawa had to agree. After the gang had succeeded in hijacking the Mystery Train and kidnapping all its passengers, their next problem had been how to get their hands on the ransom money without being caught. They had decided to use the night express to Aomori, but when they made their plans, had the rear coach already been booked by the Nennikai group? If it had, they may just have chosen Ishiyama at random and tried to force him to part with his seat, and if that was the case, it would be no help in finding the rest of the gang. The kidnappers would probably have asked him to sell them his seat on the train, but when he had refused they had killed him and used his seat anyway.

If, however, he had been a member of the gang all along, the fact that the Nennikai group planned to go on a trip the day after the Mystery Train was due to disappear may have given them the idea of using that train to pick up the money. In that case, he had planned to miss the trip all along, but either he had got cold feet at the last minute or there had been a dispute about how the money was to be split up and they had killed him. Both theories were quite feasible, but which one was true?

6

Totsugawa and Kamei searched the dead man's apartment. They were looking for clues and they started with his letters. There were quite a number of them in one of the drawers, but none seemed to provide any hints. The only one that held Totsugawa's interest was one that had been run off on a duplicating machine by the Nennikai, announcing the trip to Shimokita.

Due to an overwhelming number of requests from our members for a summer trip to the Tohoku area, and thanks to the efforts of Mr. Kojima, we are pleased to be able to announce that we will be making a trip to the Shimokita peninsula. Why not join us for four days, enjoying the wild beauty and open kindness for which this area is justly famous.

   Departure: Aug. 9 Ueno Station
   Return: Aug. 12

The letter was dated the twentieth of July and Totsugawa wondered if the Mystery Train had already been planned by this time.

He telephoned Honda at J.N.R.'s head office and told him what he had learned.

"So this case has claimed another victim, has it?" Honda said with a sigh, then in answer to Totsugawa's question, "According to Kitano here, the plan for the Mystery Train was initially submitted on the first of November last year and it was okayed on the fifteenth of that month."

"It was first announced in the newspapers in June of this year, wasn't it?"

"Yes, that is correct."

"Have you had any further contact from the kidnappers?"

"He will be phoning us again in exactly seventeen minutes at three o'clock. He is always very punctual."

"Do you think that could mean he is an ex-railwayman himself?"

"It could."

"Are they going to pay him another hundred million?"

"I think so; after all, they are a public body and their first responsibility is to the passengers. Especially in a case like this where the lives of four hundred people are at stake, I don't think they can afford to refuse."

"Yes, I can appreciate that, but it is very annoying to have to agree to the kidnapper's every demand."

"It is always like this in the beginning, but we will be able to get them in the end; it is just a question of keeping in there until we get our chance," Honda said encouragingly.

"What about the train? The kidnapper said that he would hold on to the hostages for another twenty-four hours but that he would give back the rolling stock straight away."

"That's right, he said that it belonged to the country and he would not keep it any longer."

"Did he give it back?"

"Not that we know; we can't believe anything he says."

Totsugawa put the phone down and continued to search the room. Even if Ishiyama had not been a member of the gang, the murderer had been in here, and it was quite possible that he had left some clue to his identity somewhere.

"Inspector, please come in here," Kamei called from the next room. There was a bed in the room and Kamei was pointing at a calendar that was taped on the wall next to the pillow.

"Look at this," Kamei said pointing to some figures that had been scrawled on the calendar with a ballpoint pen.

$$\begin{array}{r} 125 \\ 8\overline{)1000} \\ \underline{8} \\ 20 \\ \underline{16} \\ 40 \end{array} \qquad \underline{125}$$

"It probably means nothing, but it occurred to me that the one could refer to the one billion yen ransom . . ." Kamei said.

"If that is so and Ishiyama was one of the kidnappers, then it would mean that there were eight men in the gang altogether."

THE RED
SUITCASES

1

Honda looked at his watch. In another thirty seconds it would be three o'clock; he had set his watch to the timecast on the radio so he knew it was correct. He counted down the seconds, three . . . two . . . one . . . and as he reached zero the phone rang. Kimoto reached out to answer it.

"Well, you have had your hour," said the man in a confident tone. Honda could picture him sitting by the phone and looking at his watch as he spoke.

"I know," Kimoto answered irritably.

"In that case, I take it that you have got the money together."

"About the money, surely you must have seen the report on the news about the money found on the tracks. Now perhaps you will believe me and give back the hostages."

"Sure, I saw the report on the television, but it only mentioned that one million had been found, that is only one percent of what you claim was lost, you could easily have spread a few notes around and then pretended that you gave us all the money."

"But I am telling the truth."

"I cannot believe you, but even if you are telling the truth, it does not make any difference to us. We are one hundred million short and we want to be paid. If you don't agree, you can forget about ever seeing any of the passengers again, and it will be your fault, not ours. Four hundred people will die because you were too stubborn to pay a hundred million for their release."

"Okay, wait a minute," Kimoto said hurriedly as the kidnapper sounded as if he was about to hang up. "What guarantee do I have that you will release the hostages if I pay you?"

"You will just have to take my word for it. I don't particularly want to kill four hundred people unless I have to."

"You said you would return the train you hijacked, and yet we still have not received it. Why should we believe that you will keep your word this time?"

"You will get your train back soon; in fact, you could almost say you already have it." The man laughed.

"What do you mean, 'we already have it?'"

"You will find out soon enough, but now I will tell you what to do with the remaining hundred million and I don't want any tricks this time."

"We did not play any tricks, as you seem to think, last time. I told you before, the bag must have burst when you threw it off the train and the money got scattered over a wide area."

"Okay, okay, that is finished now. I am going to hang up, but I will call you back in five or six minutes and give you instructions about how you are to hand the money over to us."

"Why not tell me now?"

"I know that it probably never entered your mind to try and trace this call, but this is just to make it a bit harder for you to do so anyway."

2

The line went dead. Honda went to another phone and dialed a number, but he learned that they had only been able to tell that the call came from Tokyo; they had not had enough time to track it down.

A few minutes later the phone rang again.

"Now this is how you will hand over the remaining money," the man said without any preamble. Kimoto had to bite his lip and force himself to be calm in order to avoid saying something that he might regret later. They would have their chance, but for now, they could only do whatever the man said and try to ensure the safety of the hostages.

"What do you want me to do?"

"I want you to get two large red Samsonite suitcases and put fifty million in each. I then want someone to take them to the silver bell waiting area in Tokyo Station by four o'clock and await further instructions—you have a secretary named Kitano, don't you? Get him to do it, but if I see any sign of the police in the area, the deal's off and you can say good-bye to any chance of seeing the passengers again."

"Four o'clock at the silver bell waiting area, is that right?"

"Yes."

"And I am to put the money in two large red suitcases?"

"Kimoto, if you are repeating everything in an effort to draw out this phone call, then you can just forget it. I daresay that you have got the whole thing on tape, so you can listen to that. I will see you at four o'clock."

The phone went dead, but Kimoto sat with the receiver pressed to his ear for five or six seconds before he pulled himself together and put it down.

"Kitano, I want you to hurry out and buy two large red Samsonite suitcases."

Kitano ran out of the office and Kimoto picked up the phone again to call the Bank Of Japan and ask them to arrange for another one hundred million yen to be made ready for him. When he had finished that he turned to Honda. "What do you think?" he asked.

"What do you mean? About his telling you to put the money into red suitcases?"

"Yes, I was sure that he was going to tell us to put the money into sacks like the last time, but no, we have to split it in half and put it into two red suitcases. Why would he want to go to so much trouble?"

"I have no idea, I would have thought that two red suitcases would stand out and hinder him rather than help, but he obviously has some kind of plan in mind," Honda answered shaking his head.

"He said that if he saw any police there, the deal would be off. What are you going to do?"

"We will, of course, be there. We cannot afford to miss a chance of seeing the kidnapper when he comes to make his move."

Honda knew, however, that he could not do anything without Kimoto's permission. The welfare of the four hundred passengers had to come first. Once they were released, he would be free to make his arrest if he could, but until then, he would have to do whatever Kimoto thought best.

"I won't try and stop you," Kimoto said.

"Thank you, sir."

"However, I want you to remember that the lives of the passengers must take priority. I think it is fairly obvious by now that this is not the work of one man, and even if you do get a chance to arrest the man who comes to pick up the money, I want you to leave him alone. If you arrest him, another member of the gang may kill the hostages and then everything will be lost."

"I quite understand. If the kidnapper turns up, we merely mean to tail him and find out where he is keeping the hostages."

"Thank you, I am very grateful."

Honda went to the phone in the next room and called central headquarters. He told his men in the criminal investigation division to get over to Tokyo Station and put themselves in positions where they would be able to watch for the kidnapper when he made his move. He also left instructions that should Totsugawa come in from his investigations, he was to meet Honda at the station.

A few minutes later Kitano returned with two suitcases. They were both very large and very visible and Kimoto could not understand why the kidnapper would want the money to be put in something so unwieldy if he meant to try and grab them and make his getaway.

A van arrived from the bank with the money. It was then divided into the two cases, which were locked. The money alone weighed over sixty pounds, and with the weight of the cases, it would be no easy thing for Kitano to carry them on his own, even with the casters that were fitted on the bottom.

"The kidnapper told you to bring the money on your own, but you should get someone to help you carry the cases over to the station, preferably someone young," Kimoto said.

"Since he specifically asked for me to deliver the money, I think we can assume that he knows what I look like," Kitano said.

It was three-thirty, and it was only a five-minute walk to Tokyo Station.

"Would it be all right if he were to go now?" Kimoto asked. Honda looked at his watch.

"I would prefer it if you could wait another five minutes, my men should be in position by three-forty."

3

A young clerk named Tanaka helped Kitano by carrying one of the cases to Tokyo Station. They walked in through the Yaesu entrance and hurried over to the prearranged spot. Luckily it was still too early for the evening rush hour; it was all they could do to manage the heavy luggage without having to cope with crowds as well.

There was a large silver bell hanging from the ceiling near the central entrance and a sign announcing that this was the "Silver Bell Waiting Area." It was close to the coin lockers and there was also a timetable that made it a very convenient spot. Several people were standing around, obviously waiting for others.

Kitano put the cases at his feet and told Tanaka to go back to the office. The station building echoed with the sound of people's footsteps and Kitano looked around him, trying to guess where the detectives were and how the kidnapper would approach him. If the man came up to him the detectives would spot him, but if he was going to telephone him with further instructions, surely he would have been told to wait nearer the telephones. He lit a cigarette to try and calm himself, but he found that he tensed involuntarily everytime someone approached him.

He looked up at the clock. It would soon be four o'clock but still nobody came over to him. A redcap walked slowly over the concourse. There are now less than twenty redcaps employed at Tokyo Station. There used to be many more but people these days do not travel with so much luggage, and as a result they tend to carry it on their own.

The redcap came over to Kitano and put his hand on the handle of one of the suitcases.

"Shall I carry this?" he asked.

"No, that's all right," Kitano said hurriedly. "I'm waiting for someone."

"I am sorry, but you are Mr. Kitano from Head Office, aren't you?"

Kitano gave a start and the redcap offered him a slip of paper.

Do whatever he says.

Kitano looked at the man in shock. The message was obviously from the kidnapper, and although he wanted to tell the police what had happened, he had no idea where they were.

"Shall I take those then?" the redcap asked as he took the two cases. He pulled them along on their casters leaving Kitano to trail along behind.

"Where are we going?"

"To the car."

"Car? Whose car?"

"I don't know, I was merely told to go and meet a Mr. Kitano under the silver bell and bring his suitcases over to the car. I was told that if you would not follow me voluntarily, I was to show you that slip of paper."

"What kind of person was it that asked you to do this?"

"An ordinary-looking office worker type."

The redcap carried on without slackening his pace, the casters on the bottom of the cases making a loud rumbling noise as they passed through the station. They walked through the taxi rank to the car park and finally came to a halt at a white station wagon. The redcap opened the rear door and put the cases in.

Kitano looked through to the driver's seat, but it was empty.

"Hey, where is the person who told you to bring these bags here?" Kitano asked.

The redcap looked around.

"I don't know. He was supposed to wait for us here, although I have already been paid so it does not really matter to me either way." Suddenly he pointed toward the station building. "That's the man, sir!"

Kitano looked over in the direction that the redcap pointed and saw a man in his thirties talking on the phone. The man was turned half away and he could only see his profile. He could not hear what the man was saying, but it could be something to do with the four hundred hostages and he wanted to know what it was.

He walked four or five paces in the man's direction when he was brought to a sudden halt by the sound of a car starting behind him. He swung around and was just in time to see the white station wagon shoot out of the car park and into the street. The man sitting behind the wheel was none other than the redcap who had brought him over to the car.

"*Wait!*" he cried.

4

The police soon set up check points around the station, but Kitano had only been able to remember the last two digits of the license plate, so it was a hopeless task. However, they knew for sure that it was a white Skyline wagon, so they kept up the search.

They checked with the redcap office and found that although there were presently sixteen of them working there, none of them had come over to the silver bell and taken the cases to the car. The man had been an impostor.

"Come to think of it," Kitano said to Totsugawa, who had hurried over as soon as he heard what had happened, "he was a young man in his thirties and that should have made me more suspicious to begin with."

Tokyo is a very large station and it takes about ten minutes to go from the bullet train tracks to the Sobu line that runs underground there; the price for one piece of luggage is set at two hundred and fifty yen and this is too cheap to attract young people. The result is that the average age of the redcaps rises annually and it is now about fifty.

"I knew very well that there were no redcaps of his age left. I should have been more on my guard, but I was worrying about the hostages and it never occurred to me that the kidnapper would disguise himself like that."

Although the police were fairly positive that there were some railwaymen in the gang, Kitano had been unable to bring himself to believe it, and so it had been fairly easy for the kidnappers to fool him with a uniform. They may well have known he felt this way, and that might have been the reason why they had chosen him to deliver the money.

"But at least you got a good look at the face of one of the kidnappers and talked to him," said Totsugawa in an effort to cheer him up.

"But that is the whole point, I was convinced that he was a real redcap and did not pay much attention to him. I was too busy looking around for the man who had given him his orders."

"Have you got the piece of paper that he showed you?"

"Yes, here it is," Kitano said, removing it from his pocket and giving it to Totsugawa. It was written with a ballpoint pen.

"It is a very distinctive handwriting," Totsugawa said thoughtfully.

"Was the redcap wearing gloves?"

"Yes, white gloves are part of the uniform."

"That means that there is no chance of finding any fingerprints on the paper."

"I am very sorry."

"It isn't your fault; we are dealing with a very clever criminal here, and he is not likely to make a stupid mistake like leaving fingerprints for us to find."

As the criminal had been wearing a redcap's uniform when he drove away, they had thought that there was a good chance that he would be caught in one of the roadblocks, but they were disappointed. They realized, though, that he only had to remove the hat and jacket and he would look like anyone else.

It was a little after six when the car was found in Gaien Park by a policeman on patrol. As soon as they heard the news, Totsugawa and Kamei hurried over to see it.

There was no sign of the money, just the uniform and gloves left on the seat. As they had suspected, the car turned out to have been stolen and so they were no better off than they had been before. The kidnapper had shown himself briefly but had then disappeared again without a trace.

5

"Well, he did it again. He got away with one hundred million and we couldn't do anything to stop him," Honda told Kimoto. "When the redcap approached Kitano, there was talk of picking him up, but there was the chance that he was a real porter acting on instructions from the kidnapper, so we decided to keep out of sight and watch him."

"It is probably better this way," Kimoto answered.

"What do you mean? The kidnapper got away with the money before our very eyes and we still don't know what he looks like." Honda sounded very upset.

"That is all true, but as I have said several times before, my first concern as the director of J.N.R. must be for the passengers of the train. I think we are all agreed that we are dealing with a gang here, and if you had arrested the man who had disguised himself as a porter, there is no telling what his colleagues might have done. I am quite willing to pay them any amount of money as long as it means that the hostages are released safely."

"Do you really think they will release the hostages now?"

"I don't think they have any choice. No matter how violent they may be, I really cannot see them killing four hundred people in cold blood, especially now that they have gotten what they wanted. They have nothing to gain by keeping them prisoner any longer."

Kimoto seemed to be trying to convince himself. To kill four hundred people in cold blood would be the work of a maniac, and the man on the phone had sounded too calm and lucid. Kimoto was counting on this, but would he really let them go now that he had received the ransom?

"What do we know about the kidnappers so far?" he asked.

"Well, according to Totsugawa's report, it would appear that there may have been eight of them in the gang, but they fell out and one of them was killed."

"Eight of them?"

"Yes, this is only conjecture, you understand, but a man called Ishiyama was killed in his apartment and we have reason to suspect that he may have been a member of the gang."

"That means that you should be able to find out who his acquaintances were and track down the other members of the gang."

"That is the theory and Totsugawa is following it up, but personally, I am not sure we will get very far on that track."

The door of the office opened and in walked Kitano, looking exhausted.

"I have just come from police headquarters where I have been trying to make an Identikit picture of the man I saw," he told them.

"How did it go?"

"Well, we managed to come up with a picture, but I don't feel very confident about it. As I said before, I had felt sure that the kidnapper was someone else and I had not looked at the redcap very closely."

"But you must have had some impression about him."

"Yes, that's what I used to make the Identikit of him, but it's funny, the more I thought about him, the more I felt I had met him before somewhere."

"What? You mean that?" Honda exclaimed.

"I am not sure, it is just a feeling I had. I cannot think where it could have been and I have no idea who he was, so I suppose I could easily be mistaken."

"But you managed to make a picture of him, didn't you?"

"That is just it, the nearer the picture came to completion, the more I felt that it was wrong, but I couldn't put my finger on it. It did not seem to match the image I had in my mind of the man I had met before, so I cannot help but feel that I made a mistake somewhere."

"Well, if you should remember anything else, don't hesitate to tell us about it, no matter how insignificant you may think it is," Honda said.

Kitano nodded, but he did not look very confident.

"Well, now we have given the kidnappers everything they asked for," Kimoto said to nobody in particular.

"On the phone he said that they had as good as given back the train; what do you think he meant by that?"

"I think he probably meant that the train was still on the rails. The track all belongs to J.N.R., so if the train was still on the rails somewhere, it could be construed as meaning that it was in our hands," Honda said.

This was quite true. There was no way that the train could be made to disappear, and it was too big to be moved from the rails, so it was almost certain that it had been hidden on a piece of unused track somewhere.

Honda walked over to the large map of the country that hung on the wall and looked at it. The national railways were marked in black and white lines while the private ones were shown in plain black. Apart from the lines on the islands of Hokkaido and Shikoku, all the J.N.R. lines were connected, and if the points were changed in the right sequence, there was nothing to stop a train from going to any part of the country. In fact, in some cases the national railways and private railways shared the tracks, so in theory there was nothing to stop a J.N.R. train from being driven up a private railway line. Except for the bullet train tracks, which were wider than standard, the Mystery Train could be anywhere on one of the tracks shown on the map, the only problem was where?

Could the train be hidden on an unused siding somewhere? Surely, if that were the case, someone from the area would think it strange that a night train was parked there indefinitely and would get in touch with the police or the railway. Apart from that, the four hundred passengers would be making a disturbance and that would also draw attention to the train. He just could not understand it and shook his head in puzzlement.

6

While this was going on in Tokyo, Kusaka arrived back at the Osaka office from Kyoto and started to go through Okabe's desk. He was looking for something that Okabe had written so he could check the handwriting. He finally came across a copy of the draft plan for the Mystery Train. The original plan had been his, but he had had Okabe draw up the details.

Kusaka looked at the signature at the bottom of the page and compared it with the paper he had brought with him from the bus company in Kyoto. While they looked very similar and were written in the same basic style, when he looked at them carefully, he could see that they were, in fact, different. The vertical lines in the signature from Kyoto finished with a flourish whereas the ones on the signature on the plan did not. He realized that this may just be a coincidence, his own handwriting varied slightly with his moods, so he went through Okabe's drawer again to try and find another example. He finally found a postcard at the bottom of the drawer that Okabe had probably written in a lunch hour but forgotten to post. The signature on this was the same as the one on the plan, the signature without the flourish. Although he knew that he could not be totally sure that they were different without having them checked by an expert, he felt convinced that the man who had appeared at Kyoto Station was not Okabe. It would appear that the Mystery Train and its four hundred passengers had been hijacked, but if the man who had shown up at Kyoto Station was, in fact, an imposter, who were the two hundred people he brought with him and took on a tour of the steam museum? They could not have been passengers off the train; if they were being held hostage, it would be very unlikely that they would quietly go along and look at the museum without trying to get away. On the other hand, it was equally unlikely that they were all part of the gang; he could not imagine that there could be a gang two hundred strong. And anyway, the man at the bus company had said that there were a lot of children. He could not understand it at all, and he sat deep in thought.

THE
TRAIN DEPOT

1

J.N.R. had train depots situated all over the country and one of these was in Mukomachi, which is approximately halfway between Kyoto and Osaka. It comes under the jurisdiction of the Osaka office, which also runs an additional fifteen depots, but with an area of seventy acres and a staff of eight hundred fifty-five, Mukomachi is easily the largest. When it was first built in nineteen hundred sixty-one it was surrounded by fields and the area had changed very little since historical times; now, all this had disappeared to be replaced with high-rise blocks and apartment buildings as the area had become a suburb for Kyoto. The Tokaido line ran just outside of town and the siding leading into it went up in a sort of flyover over the tracks.

The night trains that came into Kyoto and Osaka from the Sanyo line and the diesels for the San-in line were all sent there at the end of a journey to be cleaned and overhauled, or just to be parked until they were next needed.

The expresses on the Sanyo line are named after stars—for instance, the Morning Star, Comet, or Venus—and so railway fans often refer to the yard as the home of the stars. Of course, many other trains are based there—with names such as the Swan or the Sea Breeze—but it is the stars for which it is most famous.

The first train to arrive in the morning is the night express from Hakata, which is known as the Morning Star No. Two. When it arrives, the electric locomotive is uncoupled and taken to the parking area in the middle of the yard, where it is overhauled, while the coaches are shunted to one side by a model DD13 diesel locomotive. After this, the other expresses come in at regular intervals, and by midday eleven expresses have come to be overhauled and it is a splendid sight to see them all lined up next to each other.

Once the coaches have been uncoupled, they are first taken to be washed in what is basically a giant car wash similar to those found in local gas stations only bigger. There are two of these, one on the east and the other on the west side of the yard, and the trains go through these at approximately twenty miles per hour. The wash is divided into three sections, first the train is sprayed with chemicals, then water, and finally it goes through some rotating brushes—the whole operation only taking about twenty seconds per carriage.

After this has been completed, one of three teams give the train a thorough inspection and grease up all the moving parts. This is all done while the train is moving slowly over the yard. If any carriage is considered unsafe, it is uncoupled from the train and another is brought up to take its place. Three trains are in the throes of being checked at any one time, and as they are continually on the move it means that there is a fair amount of risk involved in the job.

Once all the carriages have been passed for service, the train goes out of the yard to start its next journey, but that is not to say that work in the yard stops. Trains from the San-in line are constantly arriving at the yard and the work goes on through the night.

A private company is used to change the sheets on the bunks and to check that the ashtrays were all emptied. One of the workers was walking down the Comet No. 3, putting out new pillows, when he noticed something shiny under one of the seats. He bent down and picked it up to find that it was a season ticket cum business card holder; it had been the clear plastic over the ticket that had first attracted his attention.

He looked inside and saw that in addition to a Tokyo train ticket, it also contained a bank card and several business cards. Fifteen of the business cards were the same:

Kenichi Tsuyama
Editor
RYOSO MONTHLY

The train ticket and the bank card were also in the same name, but for some reason, one of the cards had been bent in half and was protruding slightly from the case. The man took it out and unfolded it to find that a note had been scribbled on the back.

Whoever finds this, please get in touch with Yukiko Norikane.

This note was followed by a Tokyo telephone number.

2

The man who found the case was named Hideo Ishidate, he was twenty-one years old and in his third year at the university in Osaka. If he had been employed by J.N.R., he would probably have just handed the case over to his superior where it would have been treated like any other piece of lost property, but he was only working for the cleaning company in his spare time to earn a bit of money, and the cryptic note on the back of the card caught his interest. He put the card with the note in the pocket of his overalls and then handed the case in to the supervisor.

When he got off work at six o'clock, he went back to his apartment and dialed the number on the back of the card. It was just after seven P.M. when he rang and he was able to catch Yukiko at home; when she heard the reason for his call, she sounded very perplexed.

"You say that you found Mr. Tsuyama's card in Osaka?" she asked, seemingly unable to believe what he had told her.

"No, not Osaka, in the carriage of a night train at a maintenance yard near Osaka."

"Oh, you mean you found it in the Mystery Train?" she asked, her voice rising. This time it was Ishidate's turn to feel perplexed.

"No, it was in a carriage belonging to the Comet number three."

"Comet . . . ? Oh, you mean the express that runs between Kyushu and Osaka?"

"Yes, it runs down the Nippo line via Oita and Miyazaki to Miyakonojo. I found it on the train that came in from Kyushu this morning."

"But Mr. Tsuyama left on a train out of Tokyo Station the night before last."

"That's strange."

"It certainly is!"

"Anyway, I found this card in his card holder with your telephone number on the back and a message asking me to ring you."

"What's the time? Seven?"

"Eight minutes past."

"Okay, I will come down right away."

"What? Tonight?"

"Yes, I should still be able to catch a bullet train down there tonight. It is important that I speak to you as soon as possible."

"I have just finished work and I am exhausted, wouldn't tomorrow do?"

"I am sorry, but a man's life might be at stake. I will pay you for your time, but it is vital that I see you right away."

"Okay, if it is that important I will wait for you at New Osaka Station."

3

Yukiko managed to catch the seven twenty-four bullet train from Tokyo Station, which was due to arrive at New Osaka Station at ten thirty-four. She still could not really understand what had happened; all she knew for sure was:

a. Tsuyama had boarded the Mystery Train that left Tokyo Station at around midnight on the night of the eighth.

b. She had not heard anything from Tsuyama and the Mystery Train seemed to have disappeared, although the railways had put out some story about the passengers requesting that the train visit Yamaguchi and so its return had been delayed by one day.

c. She had had a call from a young man who told her that he cleaned trains as a part-time job and that while he was at work he had found Tsuyama's card holder on a train from Kyushu with a message in it for whoever found it to get in touch with her immediately.

She sat back in her seat and tried to think of some set of circumstances that would bring these three facts together, but all she could think of was that something terrible had happened and she could not even begin to guess what it might be.

She was just passing Yokohama Station when it occurred to her to telephone Aoki, the deputy stationmaster at Tokyo Station. She felt sure that he would know something and would be able to help her in some way. She called him from the pay phone on the train and luckily she was able to get through without much delay. She did not waste any time and told him everything that she had heard from Ishidate.

"I realize that something must have happened and that my colleague is in some kind of trouble, and I wondered if you could tell me what it was."

"You say he was on the Mystery Train?"

"Yes, can you tell me what has happened to it and to its passengers?"

"Have you told anyone else about your colleague's card being found?"

"No, I am on my way to Osaka at the moment to see the card for myself and talk to the man who found it."

"I see . . ." Aoki said thoughtfully, then he added hurriedly, "I will check things out on this end and see what I can find out."

"But what about the Mystery Train?" Yukiko asked again, but it was too late, the line had already gone dead. She stood in the phone booth and tried to work out what his reaction could mean, but she could only guess that he had thought of something and gone to check it out. But what could have happened?

4

It was seven forty-eight when Aoki telephoned the director's office and told them what he had learned from Yukiko. When they heard the news, Kitano and Honda became quite excited and Kitano pointed out the position of the Mukomachi yard for Honda on the large map on the wall.

"So it is situated between Kyoto and Osaka and as the Mystery Train was originally headed for Kyoto, that would be the perfect spot for it to turn up," Honda said.

"The only problem, though, is that it was found in a carriage belonging to the Comet number three, which left Osaka station at seven-fifty this evening," Kitano replied with a frown.

"That's true, I wonder what it all means?"

"Anyway, I think I had better get straight down to Mukomachi yard and check it out," Kitano said, turning to Kimoto.

"In that case, please take Detective Totsugawa with you," Honda said. "This is the first real lead we have had so far."

Kitano and Totsugawa met on the platform at Tokyo Station and caught the ten-twelve train, which was the last bullet train to leave for Osaka that day. They were both exhausted but were so excited by this new lead that neither could sleep.

"If the carriage in which the card holder was found had belonged to the Mystery Train, it would mean that the kidnapper had kept his promise to return the rolling stock after all," Totsugawa said as they stood in the buffet drinking their second cup of coffee.

"But it cannot be the Mystery Train," Kitano replied. "It was found on the Comet number three, which arrived in Osaka this morning and then left again tonight after an inspection and overhaul."

"But then how do you explain the fact that the property of one of the passengers from the Mystery Train was found on it?"

"I have absolutely no idea," Kitano replied frankly. He had been tempted to make a joke of it and say that that was the real mystery behind the train, but with the fate of the four hundred passengers still unaccounted for, it would not be in very good taste. "You did not learn anything more about the man who was killed, Seiji Ishiyama, did you?"

"Kamei and the others are still working on it, but they have not been able to come up with anything yet. We still don't know if he was a part of the gang and fell out with the others or whether he was just an innocent bystander who they killed after he refused to help them."

"But you believe that he was part of the gang, don't you?"

"Yes, to be quite honest, I would like to think so." He paused for a moment. "If he was, it would mean that we may be able to find out something about the rest of the gang by checking up on his past. But about that girl who got in touch with stationmaster Aoki, Yukiko Norikane was it? How much does she know about this case?"

"I am afraid I don't know. I think she guesses that something has happened to the train; she knows it never arrived at Tottori."

"You said she was a writer for a magazine, didn't you?"

"Yes, she works for a monthly travel magazine called *Ryoso*, but even if she is on to something, the next issue does not come out until the twentieth, and so she won't be able to break the news. We managed to postpone announcing what had happened by saying that we had extended the journey for one more day, but if the passengers are not back by nine-thirty tomorrow morning, we won't be able to keep it secret any longer, that is the deadline."

"Only twelve more hours . . ." Totsugawa said to himself and then ordered another cup of coffee in an effort to keep alert.

5

Yukiko's train arrived at New Osaka Station a little after ten-thirty. Looking around the platform she saw a tall, skinny young man standing to one side, holding a white handkerchief in his hand as they had arranged.

"Mr. Ishidate?" she asked, and the young man put his handkerchief back in his pocket.

"Yes; you are Ms. Norikane?"

"Yes, that is right, thank you very much for phoning me like that."

"You're very beautiful."

"I beg your pardon?"

"Oh, sorry. It is just that I was standing here wondering what kind of person you would be and I was very relieved to find that you were so young and beautiful."

Yukiko could not help but laugh at his artlessness. She could almost see the look that would have come on his face if she had turned out to be a fat middle-aged woman.

"Could you show me Mr. Tsuyama's card, please?" Yukiko asked, still standing on the platform.

Ishidate hurriedly produced the folded card and offered it to her. She opened it out and looked at it. It was definitely one of Tsuyama's business cards and, looking on the back, she could tell at a glance that it was his handwriting, but what had he meant by his cryptic message to her? He was a professional writer and surely if something had happened, he would have tried to tell her what it was, but the fact that he had not done so must have meant that nothing had actually happened when he wrote it, he had just felt that something was about to. He must have been suspicious of something and had only had time to write this brief note and hide it in his card holder under his bunk before whatever it was happened.

"Anyway, take this," she said, and offered him ten thousand yen. He took it without a moment's hesitation.

"Are you sure that it is all right?"

"Of course, just think of it as payment for your having helped me with my research on a story. In return, though, I want you to answer some questions for me. Have you heard of the Mystery Train?"

"Yes, I have heard the name, but I don't know any details about it."

"But you work at the Mukomachi yard, which is under the control of the Osaka office, and it was the Osaka office that organized the train."

"Yes, I know, but as I told you on the telephone, I don't work for the railways, I am just working part-time for the company that cleans the carriages."

"In that case, could you take me to the Mukomachi yard so I can find someone who will know a bit more?"

"Yes, no trouble, but how do you want to go? We could take the Tokaido line to Mukomachi and walk, but if you are in a hurry, it would be much faster if we took a cab."

"Let's find a taxi then."

6

Being late at night, the taxi was able to drive straight there without being held up by traffic, and they arrived before twelve o'clock. It is a very large yard and it would probably have taken her a long time to find the entrance without Ishidate to tell the driver which way to go.

Yukiko walked into the office and gave the man there one of her business cards. She told him that she had come to pick up Tsuyama's card holder. The man was amazed that she should have come because he had yet to notify anyone about it. However, he took her up to an office where he introduced her to the depot manager, Shimazaki. There was a large window in one wall of the office that looked down over the floodlit yard. Shimazaki asked her to wait while he sent someone to pick up the card holder and when it arrived he gave it to her.

There was no mistake, it was definitely Tsuyama's.

"Please sit down," Shimazaki said. "I am very impressed with the speed with which you managed to get here."

Yukiko explained about Ishidate and the call she had received from him.

"But if you had telephoned, we would have sent it on to you. There was no need for you to come all the way down here in person."

"Once I heard about it, I just could not wait. Do you know about the Mystery Train?"

"Yes, of course, it set off from this depot, you know."

"Well, the Tsuyama who lost this card holder was one of the passengers on it."

"Oh?" Shimazaki said in surprise. "But I thought it was found on the Comet number three."

"Where is the Mystery Train at the moment?"

"Well, I heard that the passengers decided that they wanted

to see the steam locomotives on the Yamaguchi line, so its schedule was changed to fit in the trip down there. It should presently be on its way back to Tokyo."

"Do you really believe that story?" Yukiko asked. She wondered if he knew more than he was saying and was trying to cover up something.

"Well, that is what I heard," he answered with a shrug.

"What has happened to the train where the card holder was found?"

"It was scheduled to leave Osaka Station at nineteen fifty-seven, so I would say that it would be somewhere around Hiroshima at the moment."

"About the Mystery Train . . ."

At that moment the phone on Shimazaki's desk rang.

"Excuse me a moment," he said and picked up the receiver. She could not tell what was being discussed, but at one point he gave her a sharp glance and said, "Yes, she is here." He spoke for a few more minutes and then hung up.

"Was that about me?" Yukiko asked.

"Yes, I was told to ask you to remain here for a short while."

"Who was it from?"

"A man from the main office in Tokyo named Kitano. He is on his way here at the moment with a Detective Totsugawa."

"A detective . . . ?" She did not know what it could mean, but she guessed that there was more to this than met the eye.

About fifteen minutes later the two men were shown into the office and introduced to her.

"So something has happened to the Mystery Train," she said.

Totsugawa and Kitano exchanged glances; they did not know how much they could tell her. It was Kitano who answered.

"It is true that something has come up, but we are trying to sort it out as quickly as possible. We would appreciate any help you could give us."

"But how can I help if you won't tell me what has happened?"

"I am sorry, but we are not at liberty to discuss it with you. I can only promise that you will be the first to know as soon as we learn anything, that is the best I can do."

"What if I manage to find out what it is on my own?"

"That cannot be helped."

"Okay, in that case, what do you want to know?"

7

"Well, first of all, we would appreciate it if you could show us the card that was found," Totsugawa said, and Yukiko produced the folded card.

"I suppose Aoki at Tokyo Station tipped you off, didn't he?"

Totsugawa did not make any comment and just studied the writing on the back of the card.

"This is definitely Mr. Tsuyama's writing, is it?"

"Yes, without a doubt."

"Why do you think he chose to be so cryptic instead of telling you what had happened?"

"I don't know, but I think that when he wrote the note nothing had actually happened yet."

"I see, you mean he thought something was going to happen, so he wrote this note and hid it under the bunk in his ticket holder? The only question is, where is Mr. Tsuyama now . . . ?"

"So something *has* happened to the Mystery Train! What is it?"

Kitano gave her a good hard look.

"So you really don't know anything at all?"

"No, but I am afraid I did not believe that the train would be going to Yamaguchi to look at the locomotives there."

"I can see that we weren't as clever as we thought," Kitano

said, but he did not seem to show any inclination to tell her any more.

"We would like to look around the yard, if we may?" Totsugawa said.

"I will go, too," Yukiko piped in, but she was refused.

Totsugawa and Kitano were led down the stairs by one of the workers while Yukiko was left on her own in the office.

"What would you like to see?" the man asked.

"You certainly seem to have a lot of rolling stock here," Totsugawa replied.

"Yes, even if we only count the rolling stock for the expresses, we have one hundred and twenty-nine coaches here, a hundred and two of them are in regular service and the other twenty-seven are spares. Apart from these, we also look after a lot of ordinary carriages, diesels and electric locomotives."

"Do you have any sleeper cars among them?"

"Yes, we do."

"What are you getting at?" Kitano asked.

"Well, you see we have the problem of where the kidnappers are keeping their hostages. They could either be keeping them under guard in a hotel somewhere, or they could keep them on the train. If they were to choose the latter, what better place could there be to hide a train than in a maintenance depot? It comes back to the old homily about the best place to hide a tree is in the forest."

"Do you mean that you think they might be in one of the trains here?"

"Well, it is an idea. If they were being kept in one of the trains in the sheds, they would not be seen from outside, and if they were being fed sleeping pills, they would not be in any state to attract attention to themselves."

"But if that were so, it would have to mean that at least four or five of the kidnappers worked in this depot."

"Well, there can be no harm in checking," Totsugawa insisted.

They were led around the yard until they had succeeded in checking all the trains there. It took them two hours to complete the search, but they did not find anyone locked in the carriages.

"It looks as if I was wrong," Totsugawa said disappointedly.

"I could have told you that before we even started," Kitano said. "As I mentioned before, if the hostages were being kept here, it would mean that the kidnappers worked here and I find that impossible to believe."

"But you cannot deny that something belonging to one of the hostages turned up in this depot, can you?" Kitano did not reply and so Totsugawa continued, "Not only that, but the hostage in question seemed to suspect that something was going to happen."

"But you seem to be forgetting one important point: the card holder was found on the train that left Osaka this evening bound for Kyushu, not on the Mystery Train. That train only arrived here this morning from Kyushu, it was given an overhaul then it set off again after a short break, it had absolutely nothing to do with the Mystery Train at all."

"In that case, how do you explain the fact that the property of one of the hostages was found on it?"

They were both exhausted and no matter how much they discussed it, they did not seem to be getting any closer to an answer.

8

They thanked the man who had shown them around and made their way back up to the office.

"Did you find anything?" Shimazaki asked.

Totsugawa walked over to the window and looked out over the yard. The rows of trains, sparkling in the floodlights, looked very beautiful.

"No, I am afraid we didn't," he answered eventually.

Shimazaki guessed that he might not want to talk in front of Yukiko so he stood up and walked over to stand next to him by the window.

"Was it really no good?" he asked again, this time in a whisper.

"Do any of the people working here know about the Mystery Train or the kidnapping of the passengers?"

"No, I only heard about it myself this morning, and I did not want to upset the men so I kept quiet about it."

"That explains why they are all so calm. To tell the truth, I half suspected that the hostages might have been locked in one of the trains in the yard, but I was wrong."

"Is that why you looked in each one?" Shimazaki asked with a smile.

"Yes, were you watching?"

"Yes, I could see you from this window."

"I see. Also, I must ask you to apologize to your men for me."

"Why?"

"Well, when we were checking the coaches, I wrote a number on the side of each of them with chalk as we went along in order to ensure that we would not check the same one twice. You couldn't ask someone to go around and rub them all off afterward, could you?"

"Don't worry, that will soon come off when the train is taken through the washer."

"That's okay then . . ." Totsugawa suddenly broke off and his eyes started to glitter.

"The man who showed us around mentioned that you had a hundred and two express coaches in operation here and another twenty-seven in reserve."

"Yes, that is correct."

"But when we went around and checked each carriage, there were twenty-seven of them."

"Yes, that is correct, if there were any less, then we would be in trouble," Shimazaki said with a smile, but for some reason Totsugawa did not laugh.

"But you mentioned earlier that the rolling stock for the Mystery Train came from this yard and as that consisted of twelve carriages and a generator car, surely there should only be fourteen left, not twenty-seven?"

"That's true!" Shimazaki said, the full meaning of this suddenly hitting him. "On the eighth we were told to send out a train of twelve carriages and a generator car to form the Mystery Train, and as that has disappeared, there should be that many fewer cars in the yard."

"But I counted twenty-seven cars myself."

"But that can't be!"

"When I was talking to your man earlier, he did not seem to think that there was anything unusual so I automatically assumed that he meant that there were twenty-seven excluding the Mystery Train, but talking to you just now, it suddenly occurred to me that he may have meant twenty-seven altogether."

"That is right." Shimazaki stood and looked out over the rows of trains in the yard. "Why are there twenty-seven? There should only be fourteen. Where did the others come from?"

9

"I think it means that the Mystery Train has come back," Totsugawa said.

"But why didn't anyone notice it? Even if nobody knew that it had gone missing, it was not due back until today, and I have not noticed any extra trains coming in today. It can only mean that it was brought back yesterday, and if the Mystery Train had arrived back a day early, it would be sure to make people talk."

"Only if it was the Mystery Train."

"What do you mean?"

"The rolling stock that made up the Mystery Train was not

a particularly rare combination, was it? Twelve coaches, a generator car, and an electric locomotive?"

"That is true."

"Are there any other trains that look similar?"

"Yes, the Morning Star and Comets. They are both made up of one Kani twenty-four-class generator car, one Ohanefu twenty-five sleeping car with a conductor's room, and eleven Ohane twenty-five cars. It is useful to have several trains of the same construction as it means that we can swap rolling stock that much easier if there is a breakdown somewhere."

"And you say that eleven trains come back to this depot every morning, is that correct?"

"Yes."

"In that case, wouldn't it be possible for the Mystery Train to have come back without anyone realizing that it wasn't one of the other trains?"

"No, the Mystery Train had a head- and tailmark so that anyone would recognize what it was."

"What kind of headmark do the Comet and Morning Star have?"

"Neither of them have headmarks now, although they both have tailmarks. The Morning Star has a design based on the morning sky, while the Comet has an abstract picture of a comet."

"So what would happen if the headmark were removed from the Mystery Train and its tailmark replaced by one from either the Comet or the Morning Star? This depot is accessible from both the Kyoto and Osaka directions, isn't it?"

"Yes, that is correct; are you trying to say that the Mystery Train may have been carrying the Comet or Morning Star tailmark from the beginning?"

"I don't know, but I do remember hearing that the reason why it was late in leaving Tokyo Station was because one of the conductors was late in arriving. When he did appear on the platform, he was said to have been carrying a large parcel—that could easily have been the tailmark from one of the other trains."

"But what would the conductor be doing with that?"

"We don't know that he was a real conductor. The body of one of the conductors who was due to ride on the Mystery Train, Kyuji Uehara, was found in the Tama River. It is quite possible that the man who was seen with the parcel at Tokyo Station could have killed him, stolen his clothes, and boarded the train as a conductor."

"Please come with me," Shimazaki said, half dragging him out of the office and down to the yard. He found one of the yard supervisors and called him over.

"Did anything odd happen here on the ninth?" he asked.

The middle-aged man in the blue overalls put his hand to his forehead.

"I am sorry, I had meant to put it in my report, but it had completely slipped my mind," he said with an engaging grin.

"What was it?"

"Well, my team overhauled the Morning Star but Kataoka also claimed that his team had done it, too. To be quite frank, I thought he had just made a mistake, and so I did not say any more about it."

"You were right," Shimazaki said, turning to Totsugawa. "After the Morning Star arrives here, it is overhauled and sent out as the Comet number three in the evening."

So the train where the ticket holder had been found had really been the Mystery Train after all, and that was why the man who had telephoned Kimoto had said that he had already returned the train. They still did not know whether the man who brought the train in had been a member of the gang or whether he had just been threatened by them to do what he was told, but there was still one more mystery remaining that was much more urgent.

"If the Mystery Train returned here on the ninth, what has

happened to its passengers?" Shimazaki asked, voicing the question that was uppermost in Totsugawa's mind.

"I don't know. As I said earlier, I had half suspected that they were being kept in one of the trains in this yard, but I checked each of them myself and they were all empty. However, the fact that this reporter's card holder was found on the train would seem to indicate that all the passengers were taken off the train somewhere."

"But where?"

"That is for us to try and work out."

10

After booking Yukiko into a hotel and having her driven over there, Totsugawa, Kitano, and Shimazaki settled down to try and work out where the passengers must have disembarked.

They sat at a table with a map of the Tokaido line spread out in front of them. It was now past two in the morning but none of them felt tired; the fact that they had found the train itself made them feel that they were on the right track and they did not have any time to waste.

"I think we should start with the information that has been confirmed," Totsugawa said. "We know that the Mystery Train left Tokyo Station at midnight on the eighth, there are any number of witnesses to this fact, but the next morning it turned up here, disguised as the Morning Star. This can only mean that the passengers were disembarked somewhere between Tokyo and Kyoto."

"That means that the train stopped somewhere on the Tokaido line," Shimazaki said.

"Yes, if they were to move the train into a siding somewhere it would mean that they would have to change the switches and I think they would probably have just left it where it was after they had unloaded the passengers rather than go to all the trouble of changing the switches again to get back onto the main line."

"I don't know; if they had just dumped it on a siding it would probably have been found yesterday, but they would have wanted as much time for themselves as possible, and I think they were counting on it taking us at least this long before we realized what had happened."

"If we are to concentrate on the Tokaido line, how many stations would we be talking about?" Totsugawa said, starting to count them.

"There are a hundred and two between Tokyo and here," Shimazaki said without a moment's hesitation.

"That many?" Totsugawa said, his voice tinged with chagrin. If they were to check all of the stations one by one, they would not be finished by the time the train was due into Tokyo Station, and then they would have the press to deal with, too. If they took too long, there was always a chance that the kidnappers would get away. If the press got hold of the story, the gang might panic and kill the hostages. Kimoto had said that he did not think the kidnappers could kill four hundred people in cold blood, but that was only because he did not want to believe it. If they were driven into a corner, there was no saying what they might do.

"We cannot possibly check all the stations, but I don't think we need worry about the ones close to Tokyo; if the passengers were told to get off the train at one of these, they would be sure to make a fuss and it would not be easy to control them," Totsugawa said.

"But surely they would make a fuss at whatever station they were told to disembark."

"Not necessarily, you must remember that this was a Mystery Train, and I feel sure that the gang made full use of the fact. None of the passengers knew where they were scheduled to go, and so it would be very easy to fool them into leaving the train. The only thing is that being a sleeper, they would be upset if they were told to get off soon after they had gone to bed."

"In that case, they would not even necessarily have stopped at a station," Shimazaki said, but Totsugawa shook his head.

"I don't agree. If they were to stop the train in the middle of nowhere and tell the passengers to get off, it would cause a fair amount of panic, and also, the train is quite high and there would be a good chance of some of the younger children injuring themselves if they had to jump out. On top of all that, there is also the chance that they might be seen by someone. It would look suspicious if a blue train were to stop somewhere and all the passengers jumped out. There must be somewhere on the line where the train could stop long enough to unload its passengers without causing suspicion."

"So then we come back to a station."

"I think so."

"But surely, if that happened, the station staff would realize that something was wrong."

SIX CONDITIONS

1

"Let's try and put ourselves in the position of the kidnappers and see if there are any stations between Tokyo and here that could be used to get the passengers off the train," Totsugawa said. "It has to be a place that people would be interested in seeing and one where passersby would not think it strange to see an express train stop."

This seemed to be asking a bit too much, but they had no option but to try.

"I think it will be somewhere fairly near Kyoto, because it won't have stopped there before it got light," Totsugawa added.

"I see what you mean," Kitano said. "If it was light, the passengers would be less likely to make a fuss about leaving the train."

"That's right."

"I don't know," Shimazaki said. "If it was light when the train stopped there would be the risk that they would be seen by the station staff. I don't think they would take the risk, and anyway, we have not received any reports of an unidentified train stopping at any of the stations on the line."

"In that case, it means that we have to look for a station where four hundred passengers could disembark after daybreak without attracting attention to themselves," Totsugawa said, and the other two shook their heads in despair.

"But even though the passengers did not know where they were bound for," Kitano said, "everyone who worked for the railway knew it was scheduled to head for Kyoto so the passengers could visit the steam museum at Umekoji. If they saw it stop somewhere else, they would be sure to phone the regional office and ask what was going on."

"So it must be a small station where there are not so many staff," Totsugawa said, looking at the map and refusing to give up.

"But if it was a small station, it would attract even more attention," Kitano said, stating the obvious.

The more they thought about it, the less likely it seemed that there actually could be a station that would satisfy all the conditions they had set on it. They were not talking about a quiet line that ran through a deserted countryside, but the busiest line in the country that ran through the most densely populated areas in the country.

"Let's take a break," Shimazaki said and made them all a cup of instant coffee.

The time was just coming up on three o'clock.

Totsugawa took a sip of his coffee and then, looking at the clock on the wall, said, "Okay, let's list everything that would be necessary for the kidnappers to get away with it."

2

Shimazaki had a blackboard brought up to the office, then he picked up a piece of chalk and wrote:

1. A station that the train would arrive at after daybreak, where the passengers could be unloaded without attracting attention.

"What other conditions have to be met?" he asked, turning to the others, the chalk still in his hand.

"I think there are probably not more than ten people in the gang and so they would not be able to force the passengers to disembark against their will. The passengers were spread over twelve carriages, if the kidnappers were to use guns or something to get them off the train, there would be a panic in which some of them would be able to get away, but we have had no reports of that type. No, I think a majority of the people on the train were probably railroad fans, and that if the train was to stop at some station, no matter how small, that had some special historical meaning, they would not hesitate to leave the train."

2. A station that would interest railway buffs.

Shimazaki said it out loud as he wrote it on the board, but it was obvious from his tone that he did not think there was any such place. "Is there anything else?"

"I think that even if it was a small station, it would have to be one with a long platform," Kitano said.

"Are you referring to the length of the Mystery Train?"

"Yes, the Mystery Train was made up of twelve coaches, which means that it was over eight hundred feet long. If they stopped at a station with a short platform, it would take quite a while to get all the passengers off. They would want to unload as quickly as possible so they'd use a station with a long platform."

3. A station with a long platform.

"Anything else?" Shimazaki asked. From his tone one would think that he had given up already, there could not be a single station in the whole country that would satisfy all these conditions.

"Yes, I think it would have to be one outside of a built-up area. Even if they managed to get the passengers off without being seen by the station staff, if a blue train was seen waiting at a station where it never usually stops, people would talk," Totsugawa said.

4. A station with no houses in the vicinity.

"But when a new station is constructed, the surrounding area automatically builds up, and anyway, we don't build new stations unless there is enough demand in the vicinity to justify the expense. It is impossible to talk about a station on the Tokaido line that is not in an urban center," Shimazaki said.

"I know that," Totsugawa replied. "But we are just trying to list the perfect conditions for the crime to take place. We can worry about whether such a place really exists after we have finished."

"Okay, I will try to think like the kidnappers then," Shimazaki said and stood looking at the blackboard thoughtfully. "You said that you thought the passengers had disembarked after daybreak, but what kind of time did you have in mind?"

"Well, at the moment it gets light at a little before five," Totsugawa said, "but the passengers did not get to bed until after midnight, so I should imagine that it would be around six some time."

"In that case, we have another problem to deal with. The expresses do not have a monopoly on the Tokaido line; at that time of the morning all the local trains would be heading for the larger towns. Even though the Mystery Train disappeared on Sunday, there would still be trains every fifteen minutes or so, and when it stopped to unload its passengers there probably would be several people standing on the platform to witness the whole operation. Finally, we must not forget the trains going in the opposite direction. If a train going in the opposite direction were to pass while they were unloading the passengers, that would also provide a large number of witnesses."

3

They sat looking at the six conditions they had written on the blackboard.

1. A station that the train would arrive at after daybreak (about 6 A.M.), where the passengers could be unloaded without attracting attention.
2. A station that would interest railway buffs.
3. A station with a long platform.
4. A station with no houses in the vicinity.
5. A station where there would be no one on the platform at that time of day.
6. A station where they would not be spotted from a train going in the opposite direction.

"I don't believe there can really be a station on the Tokaido line that would satisfy all these conditions," Kitano said with a sigh.

"You're right. If it meets one condition, it will preclude the others," Shimazaki added. "Only large stations have long platforms, and yet a station where they would be unlikely to be seen and which does not have many houses nearby would be a small country one with a short platform. Not only that, but the whole of the Tokaido line has double tracks, so no matter where they stopped, they would always run the risk of being seen from a train going in the opposite direction."

"But it is because there is a station that meets all these conditions that they managed to spirit away the passengers of the Mystery Train without anyone knowing," Totsugawa insisted.

"I suppose you could be right . . ." Kitano began, but Totsugawa interrupted him.

"Maybe they made the plan because they knew of such a

station, but either way it has got to exist. I am an outsider and don't know much about the railways, but you two have spent your working lives employed by J.N.R., so please find out where it is. If we can find the station they used, it will mean that we are that much closer to finding the kidnappers and their hostages."

"That is very easy to say . . ." Kitano said, frowning.

The hands on the clock were just coming up to four o'clock, which meant they had only five and a half hours left. Shimazaki drank his coffee and looked at the map that was spread out on the table in front of them. Kitano joined them and they sat gazing at it in silence for a while, then suddenly they both looked up at each other as the same idea occurred to them simultaneously.

"That's it!"

"You're right!"

4

"You mean you know where it is?" Totsugawa asked.

"Yes, and it fits all six conditions perfectly," Shimazaki replied, his eyes sparkling.

This time it was Totsugawa's turn to doubt.

"But I thought you said that it was impossible."

"Yes, but there was one station that we had both forgotten," this time it was Kitano who answered, they were both smiling.

"Well, what is this station called?"

"Shin Tarui, it is the stop after Ogaki."

"Never heard of it."

"True, nowadays everyone takes the bullet train when they come down from Tokyo, and even if they took the night train, they would be asleep when they went through it," Kitano explained.

Shimazaki stood up.

"Anyway, it is no good our just sitting here and talking about it, let's go and have a look. When you see it you will see that we are right and it fits all the conditions."

The three of them left the room and went down to where Shimazaki had left his car. Kitano explained as they drove.

"There only used to be one station, Tarui, between Ogaki and Sekigahara, but that stretch of line is on quite a steep gradient and the old, prewar steam locomotives used to have a hard time getting up it. They used to have to link two engines together and even then they could only just manage to get up. In order to solve this a new line was built in 1944 that went in a large loop inland for the trains going toward Kyoto, the ones going in the other direction were going downhill so there was no need for them to make the long detour."

"I see."

"Halfway along this new gentle slope they built a new station that they called Shin Tarui or New Tarui, but after the war, the line was electrified and the new locomotives could go up the old line without any trouble."

"So they did not need the station anymore."

"Exactly. Although the expresses and night trains still use the longer route, none of them stop at the station so there is no staff there."

"What about Tarui Station, surely that is the same?"

"A lot of local trains stop there in order to serve the commuters. The area around Tarui Station is very built up."

While they were talking, the car left the expressway at Sekigahara and turned down route twenty-one. Dawn was just beginning to break and the bullet train tracks could be seen close by. The road was surrounded by mountains and here and there were signs advising motorists to use tire chains, so it was obvious that there was a lot of snow here in the winter. They crossed a small river and the road turned into a gravel track, wending its way through wide fields. Finally the car came to a halt.

"This is it, Shin Tarui Station," Shimazaki announced.

Totsugawa got out and looked around.

"You mean to say that this is a railway station?"

He could hardly believe his eyes. To one side was a large

wooden building that resembled an old temple rather than a station, but when he looked hard, he saw a faded sign over the entrance saying "Shin Tarui Station." He went inside but there was no sign of life, just a large spider's web over the ticket barrier.

5

"It is like a station in a ghost town," Totsugawa said in disgust as he walked through the building to the tracks.

"But it appears on the timetables," Kitano said as he followed them.

There was no roof or even so much as a bench on the platform and Totsugawa walked down the length of it to get some idea of its size. About halfway down there was a slight step, as if it had been added to at some time in its history. It was a very long platform for an unmanned station and must have been at least a hundred and fifty yards from end to end.

There was only one platform and although there was another track to allow trains to pass, it was red with rust and had obviously not been used for some time. The fields on the other side of the tracks stretched off into the distance with hardly a house in sight and there was a range of low mountains on the horizon. A solitary dragonfly flew overhead. It was so quiet that Totsugawa felt that he could fall asleep as he stood.

The track that ran next to the platform shone in the rising sun—obviously it was used regularly.

Inside the station building there was a blue tin can nailed onto a pillar with a sign requesting passengers to leave their tickets in it, but it was empty.

"All the expresses pass straight through this station and most of the local trains use the other Tarui Station, but still seven trains stop here every day. As you can see, though, there aren't many houses nearby, so very few people use it," Shimazaki said.

There were two signs on the platform with the station name

written on them and these looked quite new. Totsugawa walked
back to the platform and looked around slowly.

"This has to be it," he said. "There cannot be another
station that would fill their needs so exactly."

"I agree," Kitano said. "There cannot be anywhere else that
would fill all six conditions so exactly."

"But it looks a bit desolate," Shimazaki put in. "If I was on
that train, I would think twice about getting off here."

"I think the gang would have thought of that and made
preparations to make it look a bit more inviting."

"For instance?"

"Well, as you can see, there is absolutely nothing on the
platform, but that would make it even easier for them to decorate
it. They probably had a table somewhere serving tea and a large
archway or something made out of paper with welcome written
on it over the exit. Something that would be easy to clear away
afterward."

Their next job was to look for proof of this theory. They
walked the platform from end to end again, and the first thing
they came across was an empty soda can. By the time they had
finished their search they had come up with almost forty of them
and they were all brand new. It was very unlikely that a deserted
station would have so many beer and soda cans lying around on
it. The only explanation could be that the four hundred
passengers from the Mystery Train had stopped here for a break.
Totsugawa was convinced.

The space in front of the station was only large enough for
two buses to wait. If the kidnapers had readied two fifty-seat
buses, it would have taken three and a half round trips to move
all the passengers, and in the meantime, they would have kept
the remaining passengers happy by supplying them with juice
and soda while they waited. There were no trash cans on the
platform, so when they had finished drinking, the passengers
would have just left the empty cans where they were.

The next clue was some scratches on the ticket barrier that

looked as if they had been made by wire being wrapped around it. This would seem to bear out Totsugawa's theory about a welcome arch that would have been held in place with wire. Finally, there were shiny new nails showing in the old woodwork here and there that had probably been used for decorations of some form or another.

"I will get in touch with Gifu police station and have them make door-to-door inquiries," Totsugawa said just as an express passed through the station with a loud roar.

6

Ten officers arrived from Gifu police station and were sent out to check at all the local houses. Although there weren't any houses close by, there was a level crossing and Totsugawa thought there was a fair chance that one of the local people may have seen the train from there. Meanwhile, Totsugawa, Kitano, and Shimazaki waited on the platform to see what, if any, results the inquiry would produce.

"If they did use this station," Kitano said, looking around at the surrounding mountains, "I wonder where they took the passengers and how."

"They probably used buses. It would take seven round trips with one bus though, so they probably had two, I don't think there is enough room outside the station for any more than that."

"With that many people, they must have taken them to a hotel somewhere," Shimazaki said. "But it would have to be a pretty big hotel."

"Are there any hotels that large near here?" Totsugawa asked.

"Well, there is a famous waterfall nearby that gets a fair amount of visitors, but I don't think there is one that could take four hundred guests at one time."

"Isn't there anywhere else?"

"The only places I can think of that could put up that many guests would be in Gifu, Kyoto, or Nagoya—and Gifu is the nearest."

"How long would it take to get there by road?"

"At a guess, I would say that it would take at least forty minutes."

"Well, that's out then. If they were to use two buses it would take them more than four hours to get all four hundred passengers there, and that would be too dangerous. Whatever else they may be, I don't think the kidnappers are stupid, and they would not be prepared to take such a risk."

"But if they were to go to Nagoya or Kyoto, it would take even longer."

"That's true."

At that point one of the local policeman came back leading an elderly man. He looked very excited.

"This gentleman lives on a farm nearby and he says that he saw a train stopped here on the ninth."

"What time was this?" Totsugawa asked, and the old man took out a handkerchief to wipe his heavily tanned face.

"It was about six o'clock. I crossed the tracks on my bicycle and noticed a train stopped in the station. I have never seen a train there at that time before."

"What color was it? Blue?"

"Yes, it was a sleeper."

"Did you see if it had a name on the front?"

"No, I was in a hurry so I did not stop. Was it broken down?"

"Were there any passengers on the platform?"

"Yes, it was full of them."

"Was the station decorated at all?"

The old man thought for a moment.

"Yes, now that you mention it, I remember thinking that the old building was looking very good. There was some kind of round tunnel up by the exit."

"A welcome arch," Totsugawa said, looking very pleased.

7

"Did you see any buses waiting outside the station?"

"No, all I saw was the train and the platform. When I came home it had all disappeared—the train, the people, everything."

"What, the decorations, too?"

"Yes."

"What time did you come back?"

"I just went into Tarui, it must have been about nine o'clock I think."

That meant that no more than three hours had passed between the train stopping and everything being cleared away.

"If they were using two buses, it would mean that they could only have gone twenty-five minutes in each direction to move all four hundred people in that time," Shimazaki said, his forehead creased in a frown.

"That's true."

"But as I said just now, there are no hotels large enough to hold all the hostages that close to here. The only answer must be that they used at least four buses, if they did they could move all the passengers in two trips, which would enable them to go as far as Gifu easily in three hours."

"That is true, but there is no room for more than two buses outside the station, and if they used four, they would have to park two of them on the road. But that old man used the road to go to Tarui and he says that he did not see any buses."

"As I keep telling you, there are no hotels near here that would be big enough to keep four hundred people," insisted Shimazaki.

"Couldn't the hostages have been taken to Tarui?" Kitano suggested. "It would only take about twenty minutes from here."

"But what would the kidnappers do with them once they got them there?"

"I think we are agreed that a majority of the passengers are railway fans, so if they were told that they would see both Shin Tarui and Tarui stations, nobody would think that it was unusual in the least. Once they got them there, they could put them on another train and take them somewhere where they could be housed."

"Would there be enough room for four hundred people on a local train?" Totsugawa asked.

"They could easily have booked a special train to take them from there. J.N.R. is in so much debt these days that they would jump at the chance to provide a special charter train. I would not put it beyond them to get J.N.R. to help them kidnap the passengers, and if there was a special train waiting for them, the hostages would automatically think that it was part of the tour. Tarui has trains going in both directions, so the kidnappers could easily take them to a hotel in either Nagoya or Kyoto that would be big enough to hold them all."

"I will admit that it is an ingenious idea and the hostages would be all too willing to go along with it without having the least suspicions, but if that is what happened, surely the people at Tarui Station would have a record of it."

"Of course, so why don't we go and check it out?"

They thanked the local police for their help and then made their way to Tarui in Shimazaki's car. The road continued through fields with only the occasional house, and Totsugawa could see what Shimazaki had meant about there not being anywhere large enough to hold four hundred hostages.

About fifteen minutes later they arrived at Tarui Station. This was completely different from the one that they had just left. Here there was a staff of about ten; there were some shops nearby, and there was even a solitary taxi waiting outside. The other two waited while Kitano hurried in to talk to one of the staff. He spoke for a few minutes then came back, shaking his head.

"I am afraid I was barking up the wrong tree. There were no special trains that day."

"I suppose that they did not just turn up for an ordinary train either."

"I am afraid not."

"But if that is so, where on earth can the four hundred who disembarked from the train at Shin Tarui have disappeared to?"

8

The investigation had come to a halt, but in Kyoto they had managed to find out the truth behind the two hundred people who had turned up with the fake Okabe to see the steam museum at Umekoji. About a month before the Mystery Train was hijacked, the following advertisement had appeared in one of the major local newspapers.

A Trip to the Steam Museum at Umekoji.
Date: Aug. 9, 10:00 AM.
Place: Kyoto Station, Karasuma Entrance.
Number of people: 200.
Price: ¥ 200 (lunch included).

That explained where the two hundred people had come from, and the advertisement had been taken out by someone named Okabe who was probably the same Okabe who had signed the forms at the bus company.

THE
CONCRETE CAGE

1

They had heard nothing new from the kidnappers, although now that they had received over one billion yen in ransom that was understandable. It was seven in the morning and the atmosphere in the director's office fluctuated between optimism and pessimism.

When they heard that the rolling stock from the Mystery Train had been found at Mukomachi, they became very excited and thought that it would now be only a matter of time before the hostages would also be found, but there was no word.

Next they heard that it had been discovered where the passengers left the train, but there was no trace of them after that. It was almost as if they had disappeared into thin air.

"At this rate, we will never get them back to Tokyo by the nine-thirty deadline," Kimoto said to Honda, keeping his eye on the clock.

"We are doing everything we can to ensure the safety of the hostages and to arrest the kidnappers," Honda replied, as much as to convince himself as to put Kimoto at ease.

"But we still do not have so much as a description of the

kidnappers, and we have no idea where they might be holding the hostages."

"We are, however, not at a complete loss. We now know where the passengers left the train, and I think it is safe to say that they are being held somewhere in the vicinity of Shin Tarui Station."

"But when I talked to Kitano on the telephone, he told me that there were no hotels in the area that would be large enough to hold four hundred people."

"Yes, I got the same report from Totsugawa, but we still have one more avenue of investigation open to us and Kamei is working on that now."

"What is that?"

"Do you remember that man, Ishiyama, who was found murdered in his apartment?"

"Oh, you mean the one who was a member of that travel club, the Nennikai?"

"Yes, that's the one; well, we are not ruling out the possibility that he may have been a member of the gang, and Kamei is checking up on all his associates now."

2

Kamei and a young detective named Sakurai went back to see Ota, the doctor who organized the Nennikai club.

"Good morning, I must apologize for calling on you at this time of the morning, but it is very urgent," Kamei said and bowed.

"Don't worry about it, I usually get up early and go jogging anyway, so I don't mind in the least," Oda said with a wide smile. The reception area of his clinic was still dark and quiet.

"When we last met, you mentioned that the members of the Nennikai come from all over the country, didn't you?"

"That is true; we keep each other informed of local events and travel conditions, so it is very convenient."

"Do any of the members come from the Gifu area?"

"Yes, of course."

"There aren't any from that area that run a hotel or hostel or something, are there?"

"Well, Gifu Prefecture covers a very large area. Do you have any particular part in mind?"

"Have you ever heard of Shin Tarui Station?"

"Yes, I think so, it is a small station after Ogaki on the Tokaido line, isn't it?"

"Yes, well, that is the area we are interested in."

"I'm sorry, but I am afraid that I cannot help you there. The only members who run places like that are in Kyoto and Sendai."

"How about the one in Kyoto, is it a big establishment?"

"No, not at all. I stayed there myself once; it is in the Sagano area on the outskirts of the city. It is a very small Japanese-style inn and can only cater to about fifteen guests at a time."

He opened the drawer of his desk and, after looking around in it for a few minutes, came up with three photos of the inn. As he said, it was very small.

"I took these when I stayed there two years ago."

Kamei decided to change the track of the inquiry.

"Have many people left the club recently?"

"No, I am proud to say that they all seem to enjoy being members, and we have had very few people who want to drop out."

"Have you ever had to throw anyone out of the club for any reason?"

"I cannot deny that it does happen. One of the club rules is that none of the members must do anything that might reflect badly on the club or annoy other members."

"Has anyone been asked to leave recently?"

Ota looked a bit put out.

"I am sorry but I don't think that I am at liberty . . ."

"Don't worry, we won't do anything to upset you or your members, but it is vital that we know if there is anyone."

"Well, if you insist . . ."

"Yes, it may help us discover who killed Mr. Ishiyama."

"I see," Ota said, nodding. "There is one person we asked to leave recently. You see, there are several presidents of large companies who are members of our club, and this person tricked some of them into lending him large sums of money that he never paid back. Apparently there were several tens of millions of yen involved."

"Can you tell us his name?"

"Yes, but I want it clearly understood that he no longer has anything whatsoever to do with this club."

"I quite understand."

"Well, his name is Takeshi Shiraishi. When he first joined the club, his business was very successful and he did not seem to be the type who would cause any problems." Dr. Ota sighed.

"What kind of business was he involved in?"

"He ran a bus company in Nagoya."

"Did you say a bus company?" Kamei asked, his voice rising.

3

"Yes, it was called Shiraishi Tours and he owned about twelve buses. He seemed to be very successful and the club hired his buses when we visited the Atsumi peninsula, but that was the year before last. Since then, he does not seem to have done so well and became involved in the trouble I just told you about."

"You mean he started to swindle the other members?"

"Yes, he started to borrow large sums of money from the people he became friendly with through the club, and it reached the point where they started to complain. One of them was given a check for several million that bounced when he tried to cash it, so it was decided that we did not want his type in the club any longer."

"What kind of person was he?"

"He was only about forty, he had started off as a taxi driver and had managed to build up his company all on his own, so I suppose you could say that he was a successful businessman, but he overreached himself and fell into debt. At one point he became involved in real estate and even approached me to see if I would invest ten million in some land he was thinking of buying, but I turned him down. Looking back on it I can see that it was lucky that I did."

"Do you know what he is doing now?"

"I heard that he had to sell his fleet of coaches, but he is no longer a member so I don't have anything to do with him."

"Do you know if he was friendly with Mr. Ishiyama?"

"I am afraid I have no idea."

"Could you tell me the name of anyone who was particularly friendly with Mr. Shiraishi? We would like to find out more about him."

"Mr. Takano, who has a prep school in Shinjuku, seemed to get on with him very well. Mr. Takano is also a self-made man. Please don't tell him that I put you onto him though, he might not have anything to do with Mr. Shiraishi now, I cannot tell."

Kamei and Sakurai thanked him and left, but before they made their way to Shinjuku to try and find Takano's school, they telephoned Honda at the J.N.R. office.

"This business about Shiraishi having run a bus company sounds very promising, don't you think? Totsugawa said that he suspects the hostages were taken from Shin Tarui Station in two large buses, and if one of the gang used to run a bus company it would all tie in. Another thing is that he is from Nagoya, which is quite close to Shin Tarui."

"Okay, I will get in touch with Totsugawa and fill him in," Honda said briskly.

After he hung up, Kamei and Sakurai set off for Shinjuku.

"They say that you can earn a fortune with a prep school," Sakurai said to Kamei as they walked.

"Yes, I have heard the same," Kamei answered glumly. His son was still in primary school, but he already attended a prep school. All the other kids went to prep schools and his son said that if he did not go, he would not be able to make any friends.

Takano's school was on the western side of Shinjuku Station in a distinctive round building with a large sign on the roof that could be read from quite a distance. When they reached the front gate, however, they found that it was chained and the building had an unused air about it.

"Do prep schools have summer holidays, do you think?" Sakurai asked as he peered through the gate.

"No, the summer holidays are their busiest period, getting the children ready for the school entrance examinations."

"But there does not seem to be anyone around."

"Look, there is a guard over there; let's ask him," Kamei said and called out.

The guard was a man of about fifty-five. Looking over to see what the noise was, he waved them away. Kamei took out his identification and said, "We would like to ask you a few questions."

The guard's attitude suddenly changed and he hurried over to open the gate.

"Why is the gate closed? I would have thought that this was your busiest time of the year."

"That is true," the guard replied, then lowered his voice, "but they say that this building has changed hands. I don't even know if I am going to get paid or not."

"But I understood that prep schools were one of the best paying businesses around today."

"Yes, but the owner, Mr. Takano, tried to expand too quickly and opened a chain of schools all over the country, and he ended up going broke."

"We would like to see Mr. Takano, could you tell us where we could find him?"

"He has a house in Denenchofu, but I don't know if you will find him there or not."

"Why?"

"Well, I sometimes have his creditors coming here and telling me that they had tried to find him at his home, but he was always out."

"What kind of man is he?" Kamei asked.

The guard hurried back to his room and returned holding a book.

"If you read this, you should know all about him. He gave a copy to all of his employees, but the way things have turned out, I don't think I will be needing it any longer," he said with a laugh.

It was a hardcover book with the title written in gold leaf: *A Doctrine on Education by Masashi Takano*.

There was a full-length photograph of the author on the first page followed by a lot of praise by some of the world leaders in education. The things that they had written about Takano were so blatantly flattering that it was fairly obvious that Takano had paid a large sum of money to have them written. Leafing through the pages, it appeared that the whole book had been written with the sole intention of flattering Takano. He had apparently been born a poor man, but he had devoted himself to education and along the way had managed to become a very successful businessman. He was born in 1947, which meant he was now in his forties, about the same age as Shiraishi.

"Maybe Takano and Shiraishi are the people behind the kidnapping, what do you think?" Kamei asked, his eyes glinting with excitement.

"You could be right; they both owe a lot of money, which gives them adequate motive," Sakurai answered, his eyes on the school building.

"Yes, but this crime could not have been planned by the owner of a school and the owner of a bus company on their own;

they needed someone who could drive a train. How do you think they are tied in with the railways?"

"I don't know, but I think it would be worth our time to try and find out where the two of them are right now."

"Shiraishi's address was in Nagoya, so we will just have to leave that side of the investigation up to Totsugawa, since he is in that part of the country, but there is nothing to stop us from going to Denenchofu and looking for Mr. Takano."

They took the train to Denenchofu, a very exclusive part of Tokyo. Walking through the tree-lined streets, they soon came to Takano's address. They peered through the gate, but everything was quiet and there did not seem to be any sign of life. Kamei pressed the bell by the gate, but no reply came from the intercom.

They made their way to the nearest police box and asked the officer on duty there about Takano.

"I have not seen him for about a week now," the young policeman replied. "I have heard all kinds of rumors about him though. They say that he took out several mortgages on the property and that it has been taken over by a developer who intends to build a condominium on the site. He was married, but did not have any children and I have heard that they were divorced recently. Do I know where he is? I am afraid not. I get all kinds of creditors coming round and asking me the same thing, but I am afraid that I have no idea."

4

"There is something that I would like you to do for us," Kamei said and the young policeman suddenly became tense.

"What is it, sir?"

"I want you to check on everyone who comes to see Mr. Takano. I want to know their names, telephone numbers, and what their business with him is."

"Has Mr. Takano done something wrong?"

"We don't know yet, that is what we are trying to find out."

"I understand, sir. I will check on everyone and communicate it to you."

"We'd appreciate it," Kamei said, giving him a pat on the shoulder and then they left the police box.

The sun shone brightly through the trees that lined the street and it looked as if it was going to be another hot day. This did not worry Kamei, however; he could bear the heat of summer or the cold of winter when he was pursuing a case. What did worry him though was whether they would be able to find the hostages before the time limit expired. J.N.R. had announced that the train would arrive at Tokyo Station at nine-thirty that morning, and although the relatives had accepted the previous delay without too much fuss, if the train did not arrive on schedule today, the press would have a field day. They might be able to stretch the deadline by another thirty minutes or so, but after that, they would have no option but to tell the whole story.

In the case of a common kidnapping, the press usually agreed to keep quiet about it until the case was solved, but with four hundred hostages, this was anything but common. It occurred to Kamei that it might be easier than he had originally thought to win the press's silence, since they would not want people to think that they had been responsible for the deaths of the hostages if worse came to worst, but he was not so confident about the relatives of the hostages. Not being threatened directly, they would probably make a fuss and demand that something be done straight away.

"What is the time?" he asked.

"It has just turned seven-fifty."

"So we have only another hour and forty minutes," he said, giving a short sigh.

They had the names of two suspects now, Shiraishi and Takano, but they still had no idea whether or not they were actually connected to the case. The only way they could find out would be to track down the men in question, and there just was not enough time for that.

5

Totsugawa and Kitano left Shimazaki and made their way toward Nagoya. Their discovery of Shin Tarui Station had been a great step forward; they now knew where the passengers had disembarked and what had happened to the train afterward, but they still had no idea where the passengers were being held hostage. When he heard about Shiraishi, Totsugawa was very optimistic and he felt sure that he would supply them with the key to the case.

There was no need for Kitano to stay in Nagoya, so he took the bullet train back to Tokyo; Totsugawa, meanwhile, got in touch with the local police and asked for their help. They soon found an address for Shiraishi Tours in the center of town and sent some men over to check it out. At its peak, the company had owned a building in the center of town, a fleet of twelve buses, and had employed almost two hundred people.

The men who had gone to the company's address soon came back, looking disappointed.

"The building that had housed the company has already been demolished and work has started on building a block of luxury apartments on the site."

"What about Takeshi Shiraishi, were you able to find out what happened to him?"

"No, but we did find someone who used to know him well, and we brought him back with us so you could question him directly."

"Who is he?"

"His name is Akira Kido; he used to be Shiraishi's secretary."

They brought in a thin man of about forty and explained that he now ran a small coffee bar with his wife.

"The way he used to run the business, I knew it was only a matter of time before he went bust," Kido said.

Totsugawa was not in the slightest bit interested why Shiraishi had gone out of business, all he wanted to know was whether he was involved in this case or not.

"Do you know where Mr. Shiraishi is now?"

"No, he went into hiding. There are a lot of creditors and people who worked for him who never got paid searching high and low for him, but none of them has been able to find him."

"I hear that he used to own twelve buses?"

"Yes, Shiraishi Tours was one of the larger bus companies in the city."

"Do you know what happened to them?"

"They were all disposed of by his creditors after the company went bankrupt."

"Are you sure he did not take two or three of them when he went into hiding?"

Kido laughed.

"He couldn't very well hide with something that big; no, take my word for it, they were all disposed of."

"Do you know exactly what happened to them?"

"When the business got into trouble, he sold them off, one after the other. Most of them were bought up by rival companies, but I seem to remember one of them being sold to a hotel that was going to use it to drive its guests to and from the station."

"A hotel? Do you remember its name?"

"Yes, the Shimada Hotel."

"The Shimada Hotel?" Totsugawa repeated and turned to one of the other detectives who immediately rushed out of the room.

6

The detective came back about fifteen minutes later somewhat out of breath; he shook his head.

"It was a false start, there are not four hundred guests staying there. It is true that they own a large bus and admit that they bought it from Shiraishi, but it has not been moved for three days now."

"I see, in that case you had better try and track down what happened to the other eleven buses. Mr. Kido says that he does not know any details."

"It may take a bit of time, but we will do our best."

A few minutes later the phone rang for Totsugawa. It was from Shimazaki.

"I am afraid it is not very good news, but I thought you had better know."

"What is it?"

"Well, seven trains stop at Shin Tarui Station every day."

"Yes, you mentioned that earlier."

"The problem is the time they stop. You see, the first one stops there at six-fifty."

"Six-fifty?"

"Yes, it starts from Ogaki, the next station, and although I should think it unlikely that there would be many passengers on it at that time of day, the driver and conductor would have seen the station. This means that the Mystery Train stopped there at six o'clock and they managed to move all four hundred passengers and clear away the decorations on the station by six-fifty."

"Mmm . . ."

The old farmer had said that he had seen the Mystery Train stopped at the station and all four hundred passengers on the platform at six o'clock. That meant that the kidnappers had moved all the people and cleared the platform in about forty-five minutes because they would want to leave at least five minutes' leeway before the local train pulled into the station. If it was to be assumed that they had moved them all with two buses, this meant that they could not have traveled more than about seven minutes from the station.

Totsugawa felt despair close in. There were not even any large houses that close to the station, let alone a hotel or hostel.

7

Kitano was sitting on the bullet train on his way back to Tokyo. He would not arrive in Tokyo until after ten o'clock, and he knew that unless the hostages were found by then, the station would be filled with anxious relatives demanding to know what happened to the passengers of the Mystery Train. He sat back in his seat, smoking furiously.

It seemed very unfair that although they had managed to find Shin Tarui Station, they had not been able to progress any further. They still had no idea where the hostages were being held or even how many people there were in the gang. They guessed that it would not be the work of one man. It would take at least five men to watch the hostages and make sure that they did not try to escape. Totsugawa had estimated that there were probably about ten of them altogether.

The kidnappers had managed to get their hands on over a billion yen without the police being able to do a thing to stop them, and he had handed over a hundred million of it himself. He still had the feeling that he knew the redcap who had tricked him, but he could not remember where he had seen him before. He closed his eyes and tried to visualize the man's face. If he could only remember who it was, then at least they would have a clue to one of the kidnappers, but it was no good.

Someone had left a magazine on the next seat. Picking it up, Kitano started to leaf through the pages. He knew that he could not possibly find the answer in there, but no matter how hard he tried, he could not remember anything new and he had half given up. Suddenly his hands stopped. Although he knew it was impossible, there was the answer, staring him in the face. Even though he knew that it could not be that man, there was no denying what he had seen, the face in the magazine belonged to the redcap.

He stood up and made his way back to carriage number nine where the phones were situated, but when he got there, he found that they were both being used. He waited impatiently, looking at his watch repeatedly and finally one of them became free. He picked up the receiver and dialed the number of the director's office. Kimoto answered the phone in person.

"Hello, Kitano here. I am on the bullet train on my way back to Tokyo."

"Okay."

"As I told you earlier, we were not able to make any more progress, I am afraid."

"Don't worry about, the mere fact that you were able to find the station where the hostages disembarked was a big step."

"Thank you, but the reason I am ringing you has to do with that redcap who picked up the ransom money from me."

"Oh, yes, you said that you thought you had seen him somewhere before, didn't you?"

"Yes, I have been thinking about it ever since and I have finally remembered who it was."

"You have? Well, quickly, tell me, who was it?"

"I could not believe it myself to begin with, but now I am sure . . ."

He still doubted what he had seen and found it hard to actually put it into words.

"Come on, hurry up man, spit it out."

"It was the actor, Ko Nishimoto. He was dressed up like a redcap, but there could be no mistaking his face."

"You cannot be serious. He is one of the most successful television actors there is at the moment, why would he want to get involved in something like this?"

"I have no idea. All I know is that the man who took the money from me was Ko Nishimoto, and I can only suggest that you send someone over to ask him directly."

MANIA

1

Ko Nishimoto lived in the Azabu district, a very exclusive part of Tokyo and home to many of the more successful stars. Kamei and Sakurai hurried there to see Nishimoto as soon as they heard the news. Although the actor's house was not all that big, it was very modern and typical of the kind of place favored by rich, young Japanese. There was a television camera over the front door.

Kamei pressed the button on the intercom and waited.

"Yes, who is it?" asked a woman's voice.

"Police, we are here to see Mr. Nishimoto," Kamei said and held his identification up to the camera.

The woman was silent for a moment.

"Come in," she said.

The door opened and they were met by Nishimoto himself. He was well known for his good looks and had a lot of female fans, but today he looked very pale and tired.

"What do you want?" he asked.

"It is about a redcap at Tokyo Station," Kamei replied.

A look of fear came to Nishimoto's eyes, and he hurriedly

149

beckoned them in. Kamei remained silent while Nishimoto's wife served them cold drinks, but when she left the room, he came straight to the point.

"You disguised yourself as a redcap, went to Tokyo Station, and collected the suitcases from Mr. Kitano that contained one hundred million yen, didn't you?"

Nishimoto shook his head in denial, but he was very unconvincing.

"Why did you do it?" Kamei asked, staring at him. Suddenly all the color went out of Nishimoto's face and he started to shake.

"I'm sorry!" he said and bowed deeply to them. "I did not have any choice, forgive me."

"Why don't you tell us about it; don't worry, we don't think you are one of the gang," Kamei said quite honestly.

He did not look the type to get mixed up in anything dishonest, and the amount that he must be earning as an actor meant that he would not need to become involved in a kidnapping.

"They have got my son," he said brokenly. "He was a passenger on the Mystery Train."

"I guessed it was something like that," Kamei said, nodding. "Did you know that all the passengers on the train had been kidnapped?"

"No, we thought that our son was enjoying himself with everyone else on the train, but then we got this telephone call saying that he had been kidnapped. At first I thought it was a hoax, but then they let me talk to him. He is a brave boy, but he was crying when we spoke."

Nishimoto bit his lip with worry.

"So they threatened you and then gave you instructions, did they?"

"Yes, I told them that I would pay them anything they wanted, but the man just laughed and said that he did not want my money. He told me to steal a car, dress up as a redcap, and

go to Tokyo Station. I went to the studio and borrowed a redcap
uniform from the costume department. I played the part of one
last month in a play and I think they must have known about it.
They told me to go up to the man who was standing under the
silver bell and just what I was to say to him. They told me that
if I refused, they would kill my son. I know I should have come
to see you, but I wanted to do everything I could to save my son
first."

"Did they say that they would return him if you did as they
said?"

"Yes, they said that they would return him unharmed if I did
just as they said, but they did not tell me when. They said that
if I left the suitcases in the prearranged spot and then went home
without talking to anyone about it, my son would come home
soon. I have been in a terrible state, I knew that I should get
in touch with you immediately, but I just couldn't."

2

"I understand, but I want you to cooperate with us now,"
Kamei said and Nishimoto looked relieved.

"Is it true that all the passengers on that train have been
kidnapped?"

"Unfortunately, yes."

"And my son is among them?"

"I am afraid so."

"But there were four hundred people on board that train; do
you mean to say that they kidnapped all of them?"

"Yes."

"But how did they manage it?"

"They were very clever about it."

"But what about the hostages, are they going to come
home?"

"The kidnappers said that if they received the ransom, they

would release the hostages unharmed. So J.N.R. gave them everything they asked for. We don't know if they will keep their promise though, and I am afraid that we in the police force have our doubts."

"What kind of people are the kidnappers?"

"I am afraid that we have absolutely no idea. But from the way they managed to pull it off, it must have been a very carefully planned operation."

"Where are they keeping the hostages?"

"We have got a rough idea of the area, but we have not been able to pin them down yet."

"Don't you know anything?" Nishimoto asked irritably. "I am sorry, I just cannot stop worrying about my son."

"That is okay, I understand. How old is the boy?"

"He'll be ten this year."

"That means that he is the same age as my own son, although we have a younger daughter as well."

"We only have the one child."

"You must worry about him a lot then. Could you tell me a bit more about the man who called you?"

"For instance?"

"What his voice sounded like, how old you thought he was, that kind of thing."

"I think he was somewhere between thirty and forty, very calm and calculating. He seemed to enjoy frightening me. I don't know about now, but I think at some time in his life he was used to having authority. He gave me the impression that he would not hesitate to sack someone that he did not like."

"I see, and was there anything else you noticed?"

"Yes, when I spoke to him on the phone, there was a funny noise in the background."

"What kind of noise?"

"I am pretty certain that it was the sound of a model railway."

"You mean the kind that children play with?"

"Yes, my son is a real railway fan and he made me buy him one for his Christmas present a few years ago. He has got all the tracks set up in his room and it makes a noise just like the one I heard on the telephone. At the time I thought they must have bought it to keep my son busy, but if, as you say, they have got four hundred hostages, it throws a different light on it. They wouldn't bother to spend money just to amuse one boy, so it must mean that one of the gang is a railway enthusiast."

"You say that you heard this sound over the telephone?"

"Yes, all the time we were talking, and it wasn't just one train, I heard the sound of several trains all at once."

"So that would mean that it was quite a big thing then, wouldn't it?"

"Yes, in order to run several trains at once, it means that it would need quite a number of tracks. People who like that kind of thing often build switches and stations to make it look just like the real thing. They can spend thousands, even millions of yen on it. One of my friends is really into it, and his whole living room is given over to it."

"I see, so at least one of the gang is a railway enthusiast, anything else?"

"The man I spoke to did not have an accent and I remember thinking that he must have come from Tokyo."

"So, the man who spoke to you was from Tokyo, he likes model railways, and he was used to having authority, is that it?"

"That and the fact that he was about fortyish, I think."

"I see, if you remember anything else, please get in touch with us."

"Excuse me . . ."

"Yes, what is it?"

"Do you think my son and the other hostages will come back safely?"

"We are doing everything in our power to ensure that they do."

3

Kamei and Sakurai left Nishimoto's house and went back to their patrol car. Sakurai sat in the driver's seat. Rush hour had started and the roads were crowded, so they turned on the siren to get back quickly. Kamei sat in the passenger seat, deep in thought.

"What's wrong?" Sakurai asked worriedly.

"What?"

"I asked what was wrong. I thought Nishimoto had been a big help; he was able to tell us all kinds of things about the man who called him. At least it will give us a bit of a lead."

"Yes, that is true."

"Then why are you looking so miserable?"

"There was something about Nishimoto that worried me."

"You don't think he was lying, do you?"

"No, not at all, it is just that if the kidnappers could use one of the hostage's family members to go and pick up the ransom money once, why couldn't they do it again? They have got four hundred hostages to choose from, and it is quite possible that one of them may be related to a powerful politician or someone in J.N.R. or even to someone high up in the police. When I think what they could be blackmailed to do, it makes me really scared."

"I hadn't thought about it, but now that you mention it, it is really frightening. There might be an airline pilot or immigration officer among the relatives who they could use to escape overseas."

"That may be why they have not released the hostages, even after they received the ransom."

"But what can we do? I know the passengers for the train all applied by post, so we could check them out, but it would take too long."

"That's true, but all the kidnappers had to do was to line up their captives and ask them what their relatives did for a living."

"Damn!" Sakurai said and hit the steering wheel with his fist.

"It cannot be helped, we can only do our best. But that tip about one of the gang being a model railway enthusiast might be useful, we will have to check into it."

They arrived back at the investigation headquarters and reported what Nishimoto had told them. When they mentioned that one of the gang may be a railway enthusiast, most of the detectives looked rather nonplused. One of them, however, Ogawa, suddenly started to rummage through his desk.

"What is it, Ogawa?" Kamei asked.

"Just a minute," Ogawa said, pulling five or six magazines out of one of the drawers.

Ogawa was a veteran detective of about thirty-eight, but he was a quiet man and kept very much to himself. He leafed quickly through the magazines he had found without saying anything.

"Ah, here it is."

"What is it?"

"Well, you see, I am also very interested in model railroads, although I don't have much spare money and my house is very small, so I can only afford an N gauge layout."

"I did not know that."

"Well, this is a magazine for enthusiasts, and in this year's January edition Masashi Takano's name appears."

"Takano? You mean the one who owned the prep school?"

"I think so. They give his address as being in Denenchofu, so I don't think there can be any mistake. When his name first came up, I knew it rang a bell, but it was not until you mentioned that one of them was into model trains that I remembered this magazine."

The page he showed them was titled "Layout Contest" and Takano had won the gold prize.

4

The magazine showed models of all kinds of stations—country stations, tram stations—and they all had names on them. Some of them were representations of real stations and had signs with the station name, but most of them were imaginary places with amusing names.

Takano's model was of one corner of a maintenance depot and it was entitled "M Maintenance Depot."

"Do you think this is a fake name?" Kamei asked.

"It could be," Ogawa answered. "But I don't think so. If he was going to use a fake name, I think he would have thought up something a bit more original. No, I think it is likely that this depicts part of an actual maintenance depot."

"Do you think M stands for Mukomachi?" Kamei asked, staring at the photograph. Although it was only of one section of the yard, it showed several tracks with blue trains and locomotives lined up just like the real thing. "I wish Totsugawa were here; he has just been to see the real place, he would know."

"Shall I give the magazine's publisher a call and see if they know?" Ogawa asked, picking up the telephone and dialing the number printed on the first page of the magazine. He asked for the editor and when he came on the line he said, "Police, investigation branch."

"What do you want with us? We don't publish any pornography here."

"Pornography is dealt with by the public peace section. I am calling about one of the models that appeared in the layout contest in the January edition. We are interested in the one by a Mr. Masashi Takano, the one that won the gold prize."

"Oh, yes, I remember that one. It was beautifully made. What can I tell you about it?"

"It is entitled 'M Maintenance Depot' and we wondered if the M was short for Mukomachi."

"Did you think so, too?" the editor asked sounding delighted.

"What did Mr. Takano say? I take it that you met him, didn't you?"

"Yes, I did meet him, but when I asked he said that I was wrong."

"Are you sure?"

"Yes, but one of the reporters here did a story on the Mukomachi depot and swears that it is a section of that yard."

"When did he submit the model for the competition?"

"All entries had to be in by the end of September. The awards were announced on November the seventeenth, and Mr. Takano came to the award ceremony on December the fifth."

"I suppose he took the model home with him afterward?"

"Yes."

"Did he say anything about it?"

"Has Mr. Takano done something wrong?"

"No, it is nothing like that, we just want to know about the model. Did he say anything?"

"As you can see from the picture, that model is of only part of the yard; I asked him if he had a complete model of the whole yard. You see, we will be holding another competition next year to celebrate the tenth anniversary of the magazine with a first prize of one million yen, and I wondered if he would be interested in submitting the whole model next time."

"What did he say?"

"He just smiled smugly. It was obvious that he either had a model of the whole thing or was in the throes of making one."

5

"Did Mr. Takano take the model back on his own? It must have been quite big."

"He and another man came to collect it and took it away by car."

"Was the other man named Shiraishi?"

"I don't know his name."

"Don't you know anything about him?"

"No, only that he seemed to know a lot about model railways."

"You said that there was a reporter who had been to Mukomachi and thought that the model resembled it, but did he say how accurate he thought it was?"

"Just a minute, please."

He called the reporter over and Ogawa could hear them talking together, then another voice came to the phone.

"Hello, I am the one who wrote the report on the Mukomachi depot, and I can assure you that the model was an accurate reproduction of the refueling section of the yard. He was exact even down to the smallest details that someone not conversant with the place would never notice."

"For instance?"

"You see those spare carriages that are parked on the left hand side of the picture? Well, they are lined up exactly as they are at Mukomachi."

"I see, so you think that Mr. Takano went and looked over the yard before he made this model, do you?"

"Yes, without a doubt. But it is generally impossible to get in to see the place. I was only allowed in because I was writing a story on it."

"Did you take any pictures of it that might have appeared in the magazine?"

"Yes, the story was entitled 'A Day at Mukomachi.'"

"Do you think he could have based his model on your photographs?"

"No, my pictures appeared in the February edition and I did not submit them to the editor until the seventeenth of December; his model was submitted for the competition in September."

"I see, thank you very much."

Ogawa thanked him and hung up, then turned to Kamei and explained everything that was said.

"This Takano might well be one of the gang, and he could have used his model to help plan how to make the Mystery Train disappear."

"But the Mystery Train was not announced until May of this year."

"Yes, but I don't think he made the model with the intention of using it to steal a train. If he did, I hardly think he would have submitted it to the competition. No, I think he probably made the model for his own amusement, but when they started to plan what to do with the Mystery Train, they used it to finalize their plans."

"Another thing, Kamei," Sakurai said, joining the conversation. "The reporter said that the model included all kinds of detail that could only be known to someone who worked for J.N.R., and if we agree that there was such a person in the gang, then surely they would have known about the Mystery Train since its inception."

"That is true, I don't think he knew about the Mystery Train when he first entered the competition as he would not want to draw attention to himself. I think he must have heard about the train after entering."

"I will give them another call," Ogawa said and dialed the magazine's number again. He got put through to the editor again and came straight to the point. "I am calling about that model of 'M Maintenance Depot' again," he said. "Mr. Takano didn't phone you and ask you to return his model before the award ceremony, did he?"

"How did you know that?" the editor asked in surprise.

"So he did, did he? Approximately when was this?"

"Let me see . . . I think it must have been around the twentieth of November. He telephoned me and said that he needed it urgently and asked if I could return it to him right away.

I explained that it was a strong contender for the gold award and that we would like to hold on to it until the awards were announced. I said that he would be able to have it by December the fifth at the latest."

"And what did he say to that?"

"Well, at first he kept insisting that I return it immediately, but I finally managed to talk him into waiting."

Ogawa thanked the editor again and hung up. This meant that the twentieth of November was important. The Mystery Train was not announced to the public until the first of June, but he wanted to know when the plans for it were first approved. Kamei telephoned the J.N.R.'s Osaka office and was put through to Kusaka.

"Haven't you been able to find the hostages or get hold of the gang yet?" Kusaka asked irritably.

"I am afraid not."

"Well, I wish you would get a move on, the way things are going, I am going to get the blame for it as it was originally my plan."

"We are doing our best and that is why we need your help. When did you first submit the plans for the Mystery Train?"

"Just a minute, please . . ." He could be heard searching through the papers on his desk. "Here we are, I submitted it on the first of November and I got official approval on the fifteenth."

"Had you already decided on the route and the type of rolling stock that was to be used?"

"Of course, it had to be worked out to the smallest detail or I would not have been able to get approval."

"Thank you very much."

"Is this really going to help solve the case?"

"Of course, every little bit helps."

6

Kamei had got the answer he had hoped for. The Mystery Train had been decided on November the fifteenth and then all the minor details had been sorted out before it was announced to the public on the first of June. But this meant that it was quite possible for someone who was connected with J.N.R. to have heard about it by the twentieth of November.

"Well, that settles it. We now know for sure that one of the kidnappers works for the railway," Kamei said as he hung up the telephone.

"But we don't know if he is still employed by them," Ogawa said.

"You mean that it might be someone who has retired?"

"Yes, in fact I think it is more than likely. The kidnappers did an amazing job of spiriting away a whole trainful of people, but I think they were kept very busy. First they had to get the four hundred passengers off the train and to a place where they could keep them under control, and then they had to keep them under guard. Next they had to get the ransom money off the night train—and kill the conductor of the Mystery Train and the man from the travel club, Ishiyama. I don't know how many men there are in this gang, but I feel pretty certain that they must have been pretty busy. If one or two of them worked for J.N.R., they would have had to be on holiday while they did the job, and that would only attract attention to them. If you think of it that way, I think it would be more logical if it was someone who left J.N.R. recently."

"Someone who has retired?"

"Yes, railwaymen are all like one big family and it would be easy for someone who has retired to enter railway facilities and pick up any news."

"That means that one of the gang is Masashi Takano and

another is someone who used to work for J.N.R., and it is likely that they first met through a shared interest in model railways," Kamei said and looked around the room for support.

Ogawa nodded.

"I agree. After the kidnappers got the passengers off the train at Shin Tarui Station, they had to drive the train to the Mukomachi yard. If the person who did this was one of the gang, he would have to be a railwayman who has had some experience at driving a blue train. However, if they had merely threatened the original driver of the train and had him drive for them, it would not necessarily follow."

"I don't know, even if he did not drive it himself, whoever it was had to get out of the yard without anyone becoming suspicious, so I think that either way, it must have been someone who worked for the railway recently. We had better get in touch with J.N.R. and ask for a list of everyone who has left recently, although they are not going to like it when they hear what we want."

So saying, Kamei called the director's office. Kitano was still on the train from Nagoya so the phone was answered by a young man named Goto.

"I want a list of everyone who has left J.N.R. in the last year, concentrating mainly on the Osaka area. I want to know the reason why they left and something about their character."

"Certainly, if you only want it for the last year, it should not take too long to prepare. I will get in touch with you again in about an hour."

"There is one more thing, the passengers on the Mystery Train all applied by post, did they not?"

"Yes."

"Where are those cards being kept now?"

"Well, it was a project of the Osaka office, so they dealt with the selection. The cards should be down there."

"Did the cards all have the applicant's name, address, and telephone number on them?"

"Yes, we also had them write their age and profession on the card so we could keep the data for future excursions."

That meant it was definitely worth while to check the cards, but there was no time to have them sent up to Tokyo. Kamei telephoned Kusaka in Osaka again and asked him to list all the information.

A NEW PROBLEM

1

In Nagoya, it was a race against time. The local police were trying to find out what had happened to the buses that Shiraishi had sold off, and although Totsugawa could do nothing to help, he felt himself becoming more and more irritable. It was taking too much time, and time was something they did not have.

"Haven't you managed to find out yet?" he asked Fujishiro, the young detective who had been assigned the job of liaison between Totsugawa and the Nagoya police.

"I am sorry, but we still haven't been able to learn what happened to the last three; we have got every spare man on the job."

"Does that mean that you have managed to find out about nine of them?"

"Yes."

"Well, tell me about those."

"One of them was sold to the Shimada Hotel, but you already know about that."

"Yes, how about the other eight?"

"Well, four of them were sold to two local bus companies—

they bought two each. We checked them out and they are still using them and neither of the companies have any buildings that would be capable of housing all the hostages."

"What about the last four?"

"They were sold to the N Trading Company. The buses were converted for use in the tropics and exported to Southeast Asia. We checked up on that, too, and there is no mistake."

"So that means that the nine buses you have been able to track down so far were quite unconnected with the kidnapping."

"Yes, as far as we can tell. Are you quite sure that Mr. Shiraishi is involved in this case?"

This was a question that Totsugawa was unable to answer, although from what he had learned from Tokyo, it seemed very likely that Takano had played a part in the kidnapping, and if that was so, it was quite logical to assume that his friend, Shiraishi, who was in hiding from his creditors, was also tied in somehow.

"Yes, I think so, that is why I want you to check him out."

It was almost eight-thirty, which meant that only an hour remained until the time limit expired. He did not think that the press would make much of a fuss to begin with—there had been so many special trains put on by the railways recently that the press did not bother to cover most of them—but the passengers' relatives would be another matter entirely. The train had already been delayed a day without their hearing from the passengers directly. It was only to be expected that they would become worried. On top of that, the fact that the train had coincided with the summer holidays meant that there were a lot of children among the passengers. The children's parents would probably already be converging on Tokyo Station or phoning to confirm the time of the train's arrival. They had managed to put them off this long, but if the passengers did not return to the station at nine-thirty, their relatives would cause a scene on the platform and that would be guaranteed to attract the press. If things got out of hand, there was no telling what would happen to the hostages.

The hands on the clock moved up to eight-forty and the phone rang. Fujishiro answered it.

"It is for you, sir," he said, holding out the receiver for Totsugawa. It was from his boss, Honda, who was still at the J.N.R. director's office near Tokyo Station.

"Do you know what time it is?" he asked. He was not being sarcastic, the situation had passed the point where he felt like using sarcasm.

"Yes, there are only fifty minutes left."

"We think we can put them off until ten o'clock, so we have an hour and twenty minutes at the most, though there are already a lot of inquiries at Tokyo Station about when the train is due to arrive."

"Yes, I can imagine. The train has already been delayed for twenty-four hours; they must be getting quite anxious."

"What do you think? Do you reckon you will be able to find the hostages in time?"

"I don't know. I am pretty certain that they are being kept somewhere in the vicinity of Shin Tarui Station. The kidnappers managed to get all four hundred of them away from the station in the fifty minutes before the slow train stopped there, so they could not have taken them far."

"But I thought you said that there were no hotels nearby where they could be kept."

"That is true, sir."

"Then how do you explain it?"

"I am afraid I can't, that is why we are concentrating on trying to find out what happened to the buses after Shiraishi went bust. If we can track them all down, we hope that we will be able to come up with some kind of clue. How about Kamei? Has he been able to come up with anything?"

2

"We are working on the theory that Takano is a member of the gang, and we are checking up on all his acquaintances, but we won't be able to find the hostages from this end, that is something you will have to do."

"I'm doing my best, sir," Totsugawa replied and hung up.

Time kept passing. It was already eight-fifty, but they still had not come up with the remaining three buses.

"Now that Shiraishi's company has gone out of business, it is very difficult for us to find out what he did with them," Fujishiro explained apologetically.

Totsugawa could not bear to just sit there without doing something, so he telephoned the Mukomachi maintenance depot. The manager, Shimazaki, should have returned by now.

"Oh, hello," Shimazaki said brightly when he answered the phone. "I was just trying to find out exactly what happened when the Mystery Train was returned to the yard."

"I thought you said that it came in disguised as the Morning Star number six."

"Yes, but you see we have three maintenance teams working in the yard, and they take turns overhauling the trains as they arrive, so nobody realized that there had been two Morning Stars. Also, it arrived here at about seven in the morning, which is one of our busiest times of the day. We have two other Morning Stars, a Comet, and all the normal trains coming in one after the other at an average of one every ten minutes."

"What happens to the men who drive the trains into the yard?"

"When the train arrives here it is moved around by one of our diesel shunters and the drivers are free to go as soon as they have handed the train over. Nobody gave it a second thought when the Mystery Train was brought in as they just thought it was the Morning Star. I am making inquiries, but I don't feel very optimistic. You must realize it is hell in here at that time of the morning, and everybody is so busy that they don't have time to notice anything else."

Shimazaki kept repeating himself, but Totsugawa realized that he was only telling the truth. Nobody would ever think that a whole passenger train would be hijacked and they would never bother to check who was driving the trains when they arrived at the depot. Three trains of the same construction arrived at approximately the same time as the Mystery Train, and one had only to look at the timetable to realize how busy the men in the depot must be at that time of day. Totsugawa realized that the gang probably had chosen that time to return the train on purpose so that no one would notice it. He thanked Shimazaki and hung up the phone; he realized that he would be unlikely to get any new leads from that source.

"We have managed to track down one of the remaining three buses," Fujishiro said shortly after nine o'clock.

"Where is it?"

"It was bought by a nursery school. The school has about fifty children attending it and they bought it to use as a school bus. It is the summer holiday now, though, and it is locked up inside the school grounds. We sent one of our men to check and he said that it was still there."

"Still no news about the remaining two?"

"No, I am afraid not."

"It is already ten past nine," Totsugawa murmured to himself. "Can you arrange for a car for me?"

"Where do you want to go?"

"I can't just sit around here doing nothing. I thought I would go to Shin Tarui Station again and see if I can learn anything new."

"I will get right on it."

He had a patrol car brought round with a young detective named Okubo to drive it. The car started off and hurried toward

Shin Tarui. The sun was so hot that even with the air-conditioning on, Totsugawa could feel his face getting hot as the sun's rays hit him through the windshield.

"Do you think you will be able to learn something at the station, sir?" Okubo asked as he drove.

"We must have missed something. We know that the kidnappers managed to move four hundred people away from there in a very short time; they must have left something behind," Totsugawa said, although he seemed to be trying to convince himself as much as anyone.

"Four hundred people?"

"Yes, four hundred."

"That is a lot."

"Yes, I know, but there are no hotels near the station that could hold that many people."

That was an understatement, there were no hotels at all near the station, big or small. It was nine-forty by the time they arrived at the station.

"We finally ran out of time," Okubo said. Totsugawa just nodded silently.

"What shall we do now, sir?"

"Just drive around."

"What? At random?"

"Yes."

Okubo shrugged and let the clutch out. There was a low range of mountains to one side and the rest of the area consisted of fields with the occasional farmhouse.

"Damn it!" Totsugawa suddenly shouted, and Okubo braked in surprise.

"What is wrong, sir?"

"Why didn't I think of it earlier, there are any number of buildings that could accommodate four hundred people without any trouble."

"Where, sir?"

"Look, over there, in the middle of that field," Totsugawa said, pointing.

"But sir, that is a primary school."

"Yes, a primary school. A three-story concrete primary school with a gymnasium, it would be the ideal place to hide four hundred people."

"But what about the teachers and students?"

"It is the summer holiday."

"Of course!" Okubo said, raising his voice.

"It being summer, the hostages could stay for a few days on a wooden floor without suffering from the cold," Totsugawa said.

"That's right, and it will also have kitchens so it would be easy to feed four hundred people for two or three days without having to buy sandwiches or something that would draw attention."

"Exactly! Let's go and have a look at it."

Nowadays every small town is very keen on education and Tarui was no exception. The school, standing in the middle of the fields, was a splendid building.

They parked the car a short distance down the road and walked back to the school. The gate was closed so they vaulted over it and made their way up to the building. As they did, Totsugawa put his hand into the pocket where he kept his gun.

"Stop!" Came a voice, just as they were approaching the school building.

Totsugawa swung toward the voice, his gun appearing in his hand.

"Who are you?" he demanded. There was a man in his thirties standing there, wearing a training suit, his face paling at the sight of the gun.

"I am one of the teachers here, who are you?"

"Police," Totsugawa said, showing his I.D.

"What do you want?"

"Show us around the school," Totsugawa replied without

lowering his guard. He still could not be sure that the man was a real teacher.

They were shown around the whole school and gym, but there was not a soul to be seen.

"There is no one here."

"Of course, it is the summer holidays," the man said, becoming angry.

"Are there any other schools in this vicinity?"

3

"There is one junior high school and one prep school."

"A prep school? Here?"

Although he knew that these were boom years for the owners of private prep schools, he usually associated them with towns rather than empty countryside like this.

The teacher laughed briefly.

"Yes, it is owned by a strange man who thought that a quiet place like this would be ideal for studying. Of course all the students stay in dormitories. He made his money running schools in Tokyo somewhere, but I heard that he overdid things when he tried to build a national net of schools. I think he has gone out of business now."

"What is the school called?"

"What was its name now . . . ?" The teacher thought for a few minutes and during that time, Okubo, who had disappeared somewhere, came hurrying up.

"There is a call for you, sir. From headquarters."

Totsugawa thanked the teacher and hurried back to the car. The call was from Fujishiro.

"We have managed to find out what happened to the last two buses," he said brightly.

"Where are they?"

"They were sold to a prep school in Tokyo run by a man called Masashi Takano."

"Did you say Masashi Takano?" Totsugawa asked with a wide grin. "Were the buses taken up to Tokyo?"

"No, they were taken to another school he runs near Ogaki, but I am afraid that we have not been able to find the exact address yet."

"Don't worry, I know where it is."

"You do? Really?" Fujishiro sounded very surprised.

"Can you send five or six men over here straight away, we may be able to save the hostages."

"Really?"

"I am pretty sure of it."

"I will send them right over, I will come, too. Where shall we meet you?"

"Come to Shin Tarui Station."

"We should be with you in about thirty minutes."

It was ten-thirty by the time the other detectives arrived from Nagoya, and Totsugawa guessed that there was probably a near riot at Tokyo Station by that time. They went to the prep school that the teacher had told them about. It was only a five-minute drive from the station, and when they arrived they found that it was a round building set in the middle of the fields. There was nowhere around it for children to play and Totsugawa had to agree that it was probably a good place to study. There were two large buses parked outside the building, each with the name, "Takano Preparatory School" written on the side.

"Is this it?" Fujishiro asked in a low voice as he gazed at the building glowing in the morning sun.

"I think we can be pretty sure that the hostages were brought here, and if they are still there, we should be able to release them."

"I hope they are all right," Fujishiro said.

There were nine detectives altogether, including Totsugawa and Fujishiro, and they all moved quietly up to the building. If the hostages were still being held prisoner, it would mean that there was someone in there guarding them. Whoever it was would probably start shooting as soon as he realized that the police had found them. The detectives drew their guns and released the safety catches as they slipped into the building.

They stopped in front of the elevator and took deep breaths. The building was six stories high and the dormitories were all situated of the fifth and sixth floors. If the hostages were being kept anywhere, that is where they would be, but if the detectives were to use the elevator, they would tip off the guards to their presence.

"Let's take the stairs," Totsugawa said.

They climbed the stairs silently and when they reached the fifth floor, they carefully opened the door to the corridor. The corridor was lined with doors but there was no sign of anyone.

Totsugawa stepped out and when he looked at the door, he could not stop himself from giving a short cry of surprise.

4

All the doors had dynamite fixed to the handles. Although he could not see what kind of fuse had been set, he guessed that it was wired to explode when the door was opened. He knew that they would not go to all this trouble if there was no one inside the rooms, so he guessed that he had been right and that this was where the hostages were being kept.

But were the kidnappers inside there, too? He did not think so, they would hardly set dynamite on the door when they were inside the room.

"Is there anyone there?" he called out.

If there was a member of the gang in there, he knew that he could expect a bullet to come through the door, but all that came back to him was the sound of people's voices.

"Help!"

"Is that the police?"

"Be careful, there is dynamite set on the door!"

"Quickly, get us out!"

There were men's voices, women's voices, and children's voices, all raised in unison, and it was obvious that he had found the hostages at last.

"Are you all the passengers from the Mystery Train?"

"Yes!"

"That's right!"

Several voices called out in reply.

"We will just see about removing the explosives on the doors, but it might take a little while, so I want you all to remain calm in the meantime."

He then turned to Fujishiro.

"Get the bomb disposal squad over here as soon as possible."

However, it would take at least thirty minutes before they could get there and there were two things he had to do: make sure that the hostages did not panic, and to let the people at Tokyo Station know that they had been found so their relatives would not have to worry.

He told one of his men to get in touch with J.N.R. and then went back to the door.

"The bomb disposal squad should be here in about thirty minutes to remove the dynamite. In the meantime, could you choose a representative to answer some questions?"

He heard them talking inside the room, then a man answered.

"I will do the talking, my name is Kenichi Tsuyama, I am a travel writer."

Totsugawa smiled.

"I know, we found your card on the train. It was a great help to us."

"Oh, really? I am glad to hear it."

"Are all of the hostages in there with you?"

"Yes, half of us were kept on the floor above until this morning when they brought us all down here and put us together. They said that you would probably come and find us some time today, and that we did not have much longer to wait. When they left, they put dynamite on the door and said that if we tried to open it, we would all be blown up. They do not seem to have done anything to the windows, but this is the fifth floor and we still hadn't thought of a way to get down to the ground safely when you arrived."

"How many were there in the gang?"

"I only saw five, but I got the impression that there were more of them."

"Do you have any idea where they have gone?"

"No, I am afraid not."

"What time did they leave you?"

"I think it was about eight o'clock this morning."

"Is there anyone there who is sick or injured? If there is I will arrange for an ambulance to be brought over."

"No, we are all fine."

"Was there a man among the gang named Masashi Takano?"

"They were careful not to use each other's names in front of us, but one of them was referred to as the chairman, and I think that he was the man who owned this school."

"That would be Takano."

While he felt pleased that he had been able to rescue the hostages without any of them being injured, Totsugawa could not understand why the gang had just left them and fled. Although the four hundred people would be a lot of trouble for the gang to look after, kidnappers usually used their victims as a shield until they were safe, but apparently not this time.

5

The bomb disposal squad soon arrived, along with buses to take the hostages away. Seeing that he would not be needed there anymore, Totsugawa went down to the office on the floor below.

It was a large room that was filled with a model railway. Totsugawa realized immediately that this was what Kamei had been talking about when they spoke.

There was a telephone on the desk in the room and he guessed that this was the one that Takano had used to threaten Ko Nishimoto.

Looking at the large train layout on the floor he recognized it as being a model of the yard at Mukomachi. It was identical to the view he had had from Shimazaki's office window. He could not help but wonder if they had used this when they were planning the hijack.

Fujishiro sat down on the floor and flicked a switch. One of the blue trains started to move slowly into the yard and they wondered if this represented the Morning Star.

"It is very realistic, isn't it?" Fujishiro said, but at that moment, Okubo rushed into the room, followed closely by Tsuyama. Both of them looked very pale.

"What's wrong?" Totsugawa asked, although he knew in his bones what it was. He had thought all along that it was strange that the gang would release their hostages so easily.

Fujishiro scrambled to his feet.

"The disposal team dealt with the dynamite and the hostages are on their way to Gifu Station where a special bullet train is being provided to take them back to Tokyo."

"Then what is the problem?"

"Some of the hostages are missing."

"What?" Totsugawa exclaimed.

"Yes, I counted them as they got on the bus and there were only three hundred and ninety-seven. There are three missing," Okubo said.

"Yes," put in Tsuyama, "I had not realized it before, but there were three people missing. Three out of four hundred does not really show and I don't think anyone else noticed either."

"You are quite sure that there are three people missing," Totsugawa asked.

"Yes, I checked and there is no mistake, we are three people short."

"So they singled out three people from the four hundred," Totsugawa murmured to himself. "Do you know what their names are?"

"No, we have only just realized that they are missing, but as all the passengers applied by mail, it should be quite simple to check everyone's names off against the passenger list and see who is left."

"That is true," Totsugawa nodded.

He did not know who the three people were or why they had been selected, but he had a good idea. They had been chosen because they could be used to help the gang escape.

Although the number of hostages had dropped from four hundred to three, the case was still not over and they could not afford to relax.

"I want you to find out the names of the three hundred and ninety-seven as soon as possible," Totsugawa said to Okubo.

THE THREE
HOSTAGES

1

Kimoto was very relieved to hear that the hostages had been rescued safely. The relatives of the passengers had been making a fuss at Tokyo Station for thirty minutes, and he did not know how much longer he would have been able to control them. Kitano had arrived back in Tokyo and he hurried over to the bullet train operations center to arrange for a special train to bring them all home.

"Now at least the relatives will be able to stop worrying," Kimoto said with a smile.

"You can leave the rest up to us," Honda said forcefully. "Now that the hostages have been freed, we can concentrate our efforts on catching the gang, and we will get the money back, too."

But, no sooner had he spoken than they had a call from Totsugawa telling them about the three hostages who were missing.

An air of despair settled over the room and Kitano cursed.

"Do you think they have re-kidnapped them?" he asked.

"What do you mean?"

179

"Well, they could have released the four hundred hostages and then re-kidnapped these three."

"I see what you mean, that is one way of looking at it."

"They managed to get a billion yen for the four hundred hostages, and now they could have chosen three members of rich families and be planning to get another ransom for them from their relatives. Their last plan went without a hitch; they could have become greedy."

This was true; while they thought the kidnappers had already been paid more than enough ransom, the gang might not necessarily think so and could be planning to get at least the same amount again.

"We must find out who they are as soon as possible. If they come from rich families, they are probably being held for ransom; if not, they must have been chosen for a different reason."

"What do you mean? To help the gang escape?"

"Exactly. They may already have used the hostages and made their getaway."

"The passenger lists are all kept in Osaka, so we have no choice but to let them check it out for us."

2

At the Osaka office the names of the passengers were being put into alphabetical order and Kusaka was supervising the operation. They had heard that three hundred and ninety-seven of the hostages had been released and were just waiting for their names so they could strike them off the list and see who remained.

Kusaka was very annoyed; the kidnappers had got everything they had asked for; they should have kept their word and released the hostages as promised. If that had been the case, he could have been celebrating now instead of having to do this tedious job. His main worry, however, was that the missing hostages had been killed. It was quite possible that they had tried to stand up to the gang, and that their bodies would show up later.

The phone rang and he hurried over to it. It was from the bullet train.

"Hello, Totsugawa of police headquarters here."

"Are you calling from the bullet train?"

"Yes, we have just passed Nagoya and are still checking the victims' names, but I have got the first hundred here for you, are you ready?"

"Yes, this call is being recorded so please carry on at your own speed."

He turned on the tape recorder and waited while Totsugawa read the list. When he had finished, he played back the tape three times while his assistants copied down the names and put them into alphabetical order. They then pulled out the cards from the pile they had in front of them. This was repeated every twenty minutes or so when Totsugawa called up with a fresh list. The pile of cards grew smaller and smaller. By the time they were left with the three remaining cards, it was almost noon and the bullet train was approaching Shizuoka.

Kusaka laid the three cards out in front of him and looked at them; all three people were from Tokyo.

Eiji Hoshino, 12 yrs old. Schoolboy
Seijo,
Setagaya Ward,
Tokyo.

Kyoko Hayashi, 21 yrs old. Student.
306 Chateau Kichijoji
Kichijoji
Musashino.

Akiko Nakao, 24 yrs old. Office worker.
509 Aoyama Heights

Minami Aoyama
Minato Ward.

He also had their telephone numbers, but that was all. From the information in front of him, he could see no reason why the gang would have chosen these three people out of all the others. Since he could do no more himself, he picked up the phone to call the head office and the Tokyo police to let them know the news.

3

"We will check up on these three, leave it to us," Honda told Kimoto.

Kimoto nodded.

"The problem, though, is what to do about the press. If we had managed to release all the hostages, we could have held a press conference and told the whole story, but the fact that there are still three hostages in the kidnappers' control changes all that. If the story gets out, it may put their lives in danger." He looked over at Kitano and Honda for advice.

"But after the way the relatives behaved at Tokyo Station when the train failed to arrive on time, I think the press must know that something had happened to the Mystery Train," Kitano said.

"Yes, but they don't know that the whole train was hijacked and the passengers taken hostage."

"I know, but when the three hundred and ninety-seven hostages arrive back in Tokyo, the whole story is bound to come out. They have been through a harrowing experience and they will be dying to talk about it to anyone who is willing to listen."

"Yes, but Detective Totsugawa is on the train with them and I am sure that he will have told them not to speak about it to anyone," Honda said. "Still, there are lots of children among them and they will not be so willing to keep quiet."

"But then what should we do?"

"What time is the bullet train due to arrive?"

"It should get into Tokyo in about an hour," Kitano said, looking at his watch.

"In that case, I think the best thing to do under the circumstances would be to hold a press conference and explain what happened. We cannot afford to risk the final three hostages being hurt."

"Okay, I agree," Kimoto said. "Kitano, make all the preparations for it, will you?"

Kitano picked up the phone and got straight on with the job. Honda could not help but feel that the gang was still in control of the situation and knew exactly how he would behave. Thanks to a great piece of detective work on Totsugawa's part, they had finally tracked down the hostages, but then they found that the gang had been ready for this and had made off with three of them. Although they had felt proud of themselves for having managed to release the bulk of the hostages, the kidnappers were probably glad to have them off their hands.

The press conference was held thirty minutes later in the main conference hall at the J.N.R. offices. J.N.R. was represented by Kimoto and Kitano while Honda was there for the police. The meeting opened with Kitano explaining about the hijacking and Honda sat quietly watching the reactions of the reporters.

First of all they all showed amazement, and this changed to interest as they realized what a story it would make—four hundred hostages and a billion yen in ransom, it would make the front page and could even be worth an extra edition!

"Gentlemen," Honda said. "I realize how you must feel about this story, but I must ask you not to print it for a little while longer."

"But it is the story of the year."

"What a waste."

"Do you have any idea who the kidnappers are?" one of them asked.

"We think there are seven or eight of them in all. One of them, probably the leader, is a man named Masashi Takano who used to run a prep school here in Tokyo, but we still don't have a definite description for the others."

"Do you know the names of the three hostages that have yet to be released?"

"No, not yet," Honda lied. If he was to announce their names, the press would probably rush around to their houses to interview their relatives.

"But you should be able to find out if you check."

"Yes, we are still checking at the moment."

"Will you promise to let us know as soon as you find out? We are doing our bit to help, it is the very least you could do in return."

"Yes, you have my word."

"Are you confident that you will be able to get the ransom money back intact?"

"All I can say is that we are making every effort to bring this case to a satisfactory conclusion."

"What are the chances that the gang has already escaped overseas? Recently, it seems to be quite common for criminals to escape to Hong Kong or Taiwan."

"Not very high."

"Why do you say that?"

"If they had already escaped overseas, it would not be necessary for them to have kept three hostages; also, we have already put out an alert for Masashi Takano at all the harbors and airports in the country."

4

Kamei and Sakurai were given the job of checking up on the missing hostages. They decided to start with the twelve-year-old Eiji Hoshino and took the train out to Seijo.

"I bet he lives in a huge mansion of a house," Sakurai said as they walked along.

"Why do you say that? Because the kidnappers decided to take him along?"

"Why else would they bother? They have already got a billion yen in ransom; they would hardly bother to drag a kid around with them unless he was worth a lot of money. Not only that, but Seijo is an exclusive area and there are a lot of very expensive houses there."

"You might have a point," Kamei replied, nodding.

They walked for about fifteen minutes from the station until they arrived at the address they had for the boy. The sun was high in the sky and it was hot enough to give them both headaches.

"Is this what you call a mansion?" Kamei asked sarcastically.

The house in front of them was a small, two-story building, identical to the others on the street. The building took up the whole plot and there was not even a garden. Being in a good area, it would probably have cost about thirty million yen, but all the same it was not the kind of place that would be of interest to a gang of kidnappers who had just succeeded in getting their hands on one billion yen.

They pressed the front door bell and waited, but there was no answer.

"They must be out."

Though it was only to be expected that the father would be at work, the mother should have been at home.

"Maybe the kidnappers threatened to hurt the boy if the mother did not come to see them," Sakurai said.

"Why would they want to do that? They have managed to make a lot of money and should be worrying about getting out of the country, not meeting other people's wives."

"That is true."

"I would like to know what the father's job is, though."

"Shall we ask one of the neighbors?"

They went to the next house and rang the bell. It was answered by a woman of about thirty-two with a baby in her arms.

"I wonder if you could help me," Kamei said, showing her his I.D. "We would like to know what kind of work your next door neighbor, Mr. Hoshino, is involved in."

"I think he does something connected with the airlines."

"Is he a pilot?"

"No, he is an air traffic controller."

5

Kamei telephoned the central police headquarters from a nearby police box and got through to Honda who had gone back there after the press conference.

"So Eiji Hoshino's father is an air traffic controller, is he?"

"Yes, and Eiji is his only son, but we only have the word of his next door neighbor to go by, so I think it would be best if you were to contact the ministry of transport and check it out."

"Okay, leave it to me."

"Thank you. We are on our way to check out Kyoko Hayashi next."

Kamei hung up, and nodding to Sakurai, he went outside and stopped a taxi.

"Why do you think the gang would want to kidnap the son of an air traffic controller?" Sakurai asked in a low voice.

"I don't know, but I think it is safe to assume that it wasn't for the ransom. Even if he sold his house, it wouldn't fetch more than about thirty million and that kind of money would be peanuts to a gang that has just managed to get its hands on a billion. It would not be worth the risk."

"In that case do you suppose they will use the child to threaten the father and make him do something for them?"

"Yes, I think so."

"But what good will it do them to have a controller under their power? If they want to get abroad, they will need a plane, a passport, and visas—an air traffic controller would be useless."

"That is true, but they must have had a reason, and as soon as we find out what that reason is, I think we will know what they plan to do next."

They did not know about the other two hostages, but the gang obviously did not keep Eiji Hoshino for ransom, so it seemed very likely that they were all to be used to help the kidnappers make their escape. As soon as they found out what they intended to do, they would probably be able to find the gang.

They soon arrived at Kichijoji and found that Kyoko Hayashi's address was in a large condominium near the park. They went up to the janitor's office and found a man of about forty-five sitting inside in front of the air conditioner, reading a sports newspaper. Kamei knocked on the window and showed his I.D., wondering as he did so whether the Giants would win the ball game that day.

The caretaker looked up in surprise and hurried over to open the window.

"We would like to ask you a few questions about Kyoko Hayashi in room three oh six," Kamei said.

"Why? Has Miss Hayashi done something?"

"Is she a student?"

"Yes, I heard that she went to S University."

"Does she live with her parents?"

"No, she lives on her own."

"Oh, is it a rental apartment?"

"No, they are all privately owned."

"So I suppose her parents bought it for her then."

"Yes, I suppose so."

"Do you have any idea what her parents do? What kind of work her father is in?"

"No, I am afraid not."

"In that case, can you open her room for us? She is out right now."

"Are you sure it is all right?"

"Don't worry, I will take full responsibility."

6

Kyoko Hayashi's apartment was in the middle of the third floor and the caretaker opened the door with the passkey. Inside, there was a tennis racket and clothes hanging from a rail, the curtains and carpet were in a pretty pattern; it was typical of a single girl's apartment. If they had been able to telephone her university, they would probably have been able to find out her father's profession, but unfortunately it was the summer holidays and no one would be there.

"What are we looking for?" Sakurai asked.

"I think we had better start with her letters," Kamei replied.

There were about fifty letters in the letter rack and in one of the drawers in her desk, but unfortunately, none of them were from her parents. It would appear that they kept in contact by telephone, not by post.

They found that it was harder than they had anticipated to find out what her father did for a living. There was an address book by the telephone, but it was filled with her friends' numbers; she obviously knew her home number by heart. They did not have any choice but to go through all the numbers in the book one by one and ask her friends if they knew what her father did. It being the summer holidays, they did not get any reply until about the sixth try when the phone was answered by a girl's voice.

"Hello?"

"Excuse me, but do you know Kyoko Hayashi?"

"Yes, we go to the same university."

"You don't by any chance happen to know what her father does for a living, do you?"

"Who is this, please?" she asked guardedly.

"I am a police officer."

"Why do you want to know? Has Kyoko done something?" This time her voice sounded very worried.

"No, it is nothing like that, but it is very important that we get in touch with her family as soon as possible. You don't know their telephone number do you?"

"No, I am afraid not."

"Well, do you know where her father works? We could get in touch with him there."

"How do I know that you are really a policeman?"

"My name is Kamei, I am with the investigation section at central headquarters; you can telephone them and check if you like."

"That is all right, I believe you. I seem to remember her saying that her father was a director for a big company somewhere."

"You don't remember which company, do you?"

"Let me think . . . Oh, yes, I'm sure she said it was Tajima Heavy Industries."

"You don't know what his first name is, do you?"

"No, I am afraid not."

"Well, thank you very much anyway. You have been a great help."

Tajima was a major company like Kawasaki.

He dialed the number for Tajima.

"Hello, I wonder if you could help me. I would like to speak to a Mr. Hayashi who is a director in your company."

"I am sorry, but we do not have the post of director in this company."

Kyoko must have meant that he was an executive when she said director. Kamei was not sure how he should continue.

"Do you have anyone of that name among the executives?"

"Yes, we have two people of that name."

He was at a loss again.

"Do either of them have a daughter in university?"

"What?"

Kamei realized that if they were executives, there was a good chance that they were both in their late forties or early fifties and it would not be surprising if they both had children in university.

"I want to get in touch with the Mr. Hayashi who has a daughter named Kyoko."

"Just a minute, please."

He could hear the operator looking through some papers.

"Yes, I know who you mean, you want Mr. Taichiro Hayashi in the aircraft manufacturing division."

"Aircraft manufacturing?"

"Yes, that is correct."

"Is he at work today?"

"Yes, I believe so, but the aircraft division is at our Mitaka works, so could you phone there, please?"

"We will go there in person, thank you very much."

He broke off the connection and then telephoned headquarters again.

"Hello, Kamei here."

"Oh, hello." It was Totsugawa's voice and Kamei smiled.

"Hello, when did you get back?"

"I just got in a few moments ago. Oh, yes, I've just been told to tell you that Hideo Hoshino is definitely an air traffic controller and that he is at work today."

"Thank you. I have just managed to find out that Kyoko Hayashi's father works for the aircraft construction division of Tajima Heavy Industries, which is situated in Mitaka, and we are on our way over to see him now."

"All right, in that case I will check up on the third hostage, Akiko Nakao, for you."

"Thank you."

"But I wonder what the kidnappers are up to; surely they are not planning to make a new airplane to use to escape the country."

Totsugawa said it as a joke.

7

Totsugawa forced his exhausted body out of his chair and, together with detective Ogawa, made his way down to Minami Aoyama. They went in an unmarked patrol car; Ogawa drove.

"What do you think the kidnappers are planning?" Ogawa asked.

"Well, if they want to get out of the country, they are going to have to use either a ship or a plane. I think the fact that they have kidnapped the children of an air traffic controller and a manager at the aircraft division at Tajima Industries must have some connection, but I have no idea how they intend to utilize them."

If they intended to leave the country by air, there were two ways this could be achieved. One would be to hijack a plane, but that would be very dangerous and their chances of getting away with it minimal. Judging by the way they had planned their operation up to now, he did not think they would use such a crude method.

The second way would be simply to buy a ticket and board the plane like any other passenger. They had succeeded in getting their hands on the ransom money on the tenth and at that time nobody had had any idea who they were, so if they had prepared their passports and visas beforehand, they could have left from Narita that day, but they didn't. Why could this be?

"There is one more point that I don't understand," Ogawa said.

"What is that?"

"Well, up until now, the kidnappers have planned everything down to the minutest detail."

"What about it?"

"Well, now that they have come to the final and most important bit, it seems strange to me that they should have just happened to find three people among the hostages who could help them get out of the country. I don't understand why they did not just leave the country from Narita as soon as they got the money."

"I was just thinking the same thing."

"And what conclusion did you come to?"

"It occurred to me that for some reason they were unable to leave the country on the tenth."

"Why would that be?"

"Maybe some of them could not get passports or visas."

"I see what you mean, some of them could be on probation and unable to apply for a passport," Ogawa said, his eyes glittering.

"Yes, when they made their plans, they may have agreed that they would all escape together, so the people who had passports could not just run off and leave the others as soon as they had the money."

"But if some of them are on probation, they won't be able to get passports, no matter how long they wait."

"That is why they managed to find out that there would be the son of an air traffic controller and the daughter of the manager of an aircraft company on the Mystery Train. Somehow they used this fact when they made their plans."

"But how could they have known?"

"I have no idea, but they had planned everything so carefully up to now that I don't think they would leave the escape to luck."

He had just finished speaking when the car pulled up in front of the Aoyama Heights.

THE INQUIRY

1

It was an old apartment building that looked as if it had been standing for about twenty years. A famous critic in Japan had once said that the condominiums of today would be the slums of tomorrow, and even though he lived in a condominium himself, looking at the building in front of him, Totsugawa had to admit that the critic was probably right. All the verandahs had washing hanging out on them and this added to the general impression of squalor, but even so, it had a good address and each apartment probably cost at least twenty million yen.

He went up to the caretaker's room and asked about Akiko Nakao.

"Does she live here on her own?"

"Yes, that's right," the caretaker replied in a low voice. The caretaker was an old man in not much better condition than the building, and his eyes behind his thick glasses seemed half asleep.

"We want to know something about her family, what her father or brother do for a living."

"I don't know anything about that kind of thing," the old man said uninterestedly.

Totsugawa did not have any choice, so he had the man open her door for them with the passkey.

While the outside of the building did not look very good, the inside of her apartment was a completely different story; the walls had been recently repapered and there was a pretty embroidered cloth on the kitchen table. It was obvious that she was very interested in travel and the bookcase was overflowing with books and magazines on the subject. They guessed that this was why she had decided to go on the Mystery Train.

They found the telephone by the bed with an address book next to it, but like Kyoko Hayashi, Akiko Nakao apparently knew her home number by heart as there was no note of it. The book was filled with the names and addresses of friends, but Totsugawa guessed that there was no point in trying these as they would all be at work at that time of day. On the last page, however, there was her work telephone number; she worked for the town council.

Totsugawa dialed the number and asked for the personnel department.

"I would like to ask you a few questions about Akiko Nakao, who works for you. Do you know what her father does for a living?"

When he told them who he was, he was put through to the department manager.

"Hello? Yes, her father is a pilot for a private airline."

"A pilot?"

"Yes, oh, just a minute, I am sorry, he retired about eighteen months ago, but he had worked for T Airlines until then."

"Do you know where he went after retirement?"

"No, I am afraid our records do not go that far."

"Could you tell me her father's name?"

"Yes, Takatoshi Nakao, he's fifty-seven, and her mother is Satoko, fifty."

"Does she have any brothers or sisters?"

"Yes, she has a sister, but I remember her telling me that she was married to an American and lives in Los Angeles now."

"Do you have her parent's telephone number?"

"Yes, it is 555-1234. The address is in Karasuyama in Setagaya Ward."

2

Totsugawa dialed the number but there was no answer.

"Hold on to this for a while and see if you can get a reply," he said and gave the receiver to Ogawa.

Now they knew about the families of all three hostages and they all had one thing in common—airplanes. It was obvious that the kidnappers intended to use their hostages to force the parents to help them get away, but he could not understand how they hoped to achieve this. If they were going to try and escape overseas, they would have to do it by airliner, he hardly thought they would be able to do it by military aircraft. The only Japanese airliner was the YS, which was now out of production; all the Japanese companies used foreign-built aircraft.

He could not see how they hoped to use an air traffic controller and a retired pilot to help them escape; it would probably be easier if they were just to hijack a plane. They had to have some kind of plan. When he had rescued the other hostages from the school at Shin Tarui, the kidnappers had already disappeared with their hostages, and so it would appear that they had already put their plan in action.

"Still no answer?" Totsugawa asked. Ogawa was sitting with the receiver to his ear.

"No, but it is still ringing."

"In that case, I want you to go to the address in Karasuyama and see if there is anyone there."

"What will you do?"

"I will go back to the office; they have probably got the list of people who left J.N.R. by now. If you manage to find the pilot, I want you to find out what he does now and whether he has been contacted by the gang."

"What if I just meet his wife?"

"You can still ask her the same thing."

"Okay."

Ogawa put the phone down and hurried off. Totsugawa went back to the central headquarters and made a report of everything to Honda. After he had heard all that he had to say, Honda stood up and wrote "Pilot, Air Traffic Controller, Manager of Aircraft Production" on a blackboard on one side of the room.

"I can't see what they are up to at all," he said. "How about you?"

"I think it is obvious that they intend to use their hostages to escape overseas."

"Yes, even I can guess that much, but how do you think they hope to manage it?"

"Have you heard anything from Kamei since he went to the plant in Mitaka?"

"No, not yet."

"Have you received the list of people who have left J.N.R. yet?"

"Yes, it arrived a short while ago."

He opened the drawer in his desk, took out the list, and handed it to Totsugawa.

"There have been five this year and twelve since last year," he said.

"That is quite a lot."

"Yes, it is because of all these illegal strikes they have been having. I have asked J.N.R. to check them out for us."

As he spoke, an officer came out of the information office with a magazine in his hand.

"I have found it, sir, you were right," he said with a smile.

"I thought I would be."

"This is it," he said and handed over the magazine. "It is on page thirty-six."

3

"What is it?" Totsugawa asked and Honda flicked through the pages.

"It is about the three hostages. I thought it strange that the kidnappers should plan the hijack so carefully but not make any plans for their escape."

"Yes, I was wondering about the same thing."

"That was when it occurred to me that the kidnappers may have already known that there were some people among the hostages who would be useful to them. There again, they may only have thought up their method of escape after they knew about these people."

"I thought of that, too, but the problem still remains of how they knew who would be on the train, let alone what their parents did for a living."

"Well, I think you will find that the answer is here in this magazine. Yes, here it is."

He opened it to page thirty-six and passed it over to Totsugawa.

Unique Passengers for the Mystery Train!

Said the headline and it was followed by this story.

Recently the special trains that have been laid on by the J.N.R. have met with a lot of success and the Mystery Train, which was announced recently by the Osaka district office, is no exception with twenty applicants for every seat. The four hundred passengers were eventually chosen by lot and among them were these unique people.

Mr. A, seventy-two, and his wife, sixty-eight, whose ages come to one hundred and forty.

The son of an air traffic controller, Eiji.

The daughter of the manager of the aircraft construction division at Tajima Heavy Industries.

The daughter of a veteran airline pilot.

While the parents of these three have devoted themselves to air travel, their children are all confirmed railway fanatics.

Among the four hundred there is also the young son of the popular actor, Ko Nishimoto.

"I see what you mean, the kidnappers must have read this and then decided to use them to help make their escape."

"Yes, I think the reporter who wrote the article must have gone to J.N.R.'s Osaka office and been allowed to look through all the application cards in order to get the information."

"Be that as it may, it still does not tell us how they hope to use them to make their escape."

As he spoke, Totsugawa looked at his watch; it was four o'clock.

They have probably already made their move, he thought, but not knowing what they planned, he was helpless to do anything about it.

"An air traffic controller, an aircraft manufacturer, and a retired pilot," Honda said out loud. "How can they possibly hope to use them? If you were one of the kidnappers what would you do?"

"That's what I have been trying to work out myself," Totsugawa said, shaking his head.

"First we have the air traffic controller, how could you use him to escape overseas?"

"I think it would be impossible; for one thing, controllers work in a group and having the power to blackmail just one of them would not help at all."

"I agree, and how about an aircraft manufacturer, how would you use him?"

"You don't suppose they are planning to buy an airplane of their own, do you?" Totsugawa said with a laugh. He had meant it as a joke, but Honda took him seriously.

"That might be the answer."

"You can't be serious."

"Yes, I am. They have got a billion yen, which would be adequate to buy a small plane—they could even get a medium-sized craft—all that would be missing would be a pilot and that was why they kidnapped the pilot's daughter, so they could force him to fly it for them."

"Yes, it makes sense," Totsugawa said, nodding, but then he frowned. "That would be all right if they were just thinking of escaping to another part of Japan, but they could not go overseas in it. We have all the airports in this country under surveillance, and if they were to land at any of these, they would be arrested straight away. No, from what I know of these people, I don't think they would come up with a half-cocked plan like that."

"Yes, I suppose you are right," Honda said, looking disappointed.

4

While Kitano was relieved that three hundred and ninety-seven of the hostages had been released, he now had to worry about the J.N.R. staff who had been on the train. There had been six of them: the driver and his assistant, the chief conductor, two conductors, and Mr. Okabe from the Osaka district office. All of them were from the Osaka area.

Already one of the conductors, Uehara, had been found murdered, and they knew from his handwriting that the Okabe who had appeared at the bus company in Kyoto was a fake, but what had happened to the others? There could be only be two reasons why they were not released with the other hostages; one was that they were part of the gang and the other was that they had been able to recognize one or more of the gang.

Kitano did not want to believe that six members of the J.N.R. staff could really be connected with the hijacking of the train, but he had to admit it was a possibility. They may have been approached by Takano or Shiraishi and persuaded to join in the plan. Uehara may have refused, and that was why he had been murdered and his body dumped in the river at Tokyo. If this was the case, it would bring the number of the gang up to seven, which the police agreed was a likely number, but something deep within Kitano rebelled at the idea.

He much preferred to think that there had been an ex-railwayman in the gang who would have been easily recognized by his former colleagues. And rather than let them go straight away, they had been kept until he got away. That way the police would not be able to learn the identity of the gang until it was too late. But what would happen to the hostages now? Would they all be killed to make sure they never spoke?

Kitano guessed that one of the gang had probably been a friend of Uehara's and that he had tried to get him to join in the plot. When he refused, he had been killed so news of the hijacking would not get out until it was too late. Now that the kidnappers had the ransom money, though, surely there was no need to kill the remaining hostages. Kimoto had not mentioned them at all at the press conference; he had concentrated on the fact that the bulk of the passengers had been rescued safely, but Kitano was really very worried about them, too.

5

The fact that the J.N.R. staff had not been released made it obvious that there were at least some ex-J.N.R. employees involved in the crime. The way they managed to hijack the

Mystery Train and hide it afterward, not to mention the way they succeeded in getting the ransom money off the night train, also made it impossible not to come to this conclusion.

They had drawn up a list of the people who had left J.N.R. involuntarily over the last year, and there were twelve of them altogether. The reasons for their dismissals ranged from drunken driving to rape, and Kitano knew several of the names on the list himself.

J.N.R. had a lot of problems—from their massive debt to pollution to a deterioration in service—so whenever a railwayman did something wrong, he got an inordinate amount of press coverage. It was always very painful for Kimoto or Kitano when this happened, but railwaymen were trusted by the public; so, like policemen or bankers, it was only to be expected that the press would make a fuss. The most unfortunate thing was, however, that due to the notoriety the scandal would bring, they often found it very difficult to find any other work after they lost their jobs with J.N.R.

Kitano decided to telephone each man on the list. If any one of them was a member of the gang, he would be busy trying to get away and would not be home. So if the person answered the phone himself or if someone was able to tell where the man worked now, Kitano could strike him off the list of suspects.

He had to listen to some terrible stories of suffering, and one of the men had even been driven to suicide after he lost his job, but in the end he was left with a list of four names:

Taiichi Kajima	35	ex-driver
Mikio Arai	27	ex-conductor
Tetsu Fukuda	26	ex-conductor
Ken Kubota	30	ex-mechanic

Taiichi Kajima had been the driver of a blue train, but he had also been an avid gambler. As a result, he had ended up borrowing three million yen from a loan shark, and in order to pay it back, he had swindled one of his friends out of two million yen. It had been his first offense and he had soon paid back the money, so the police did not prosecute, but he had been forced to resign and the scandal in the press had even resulted in his wife leaving him.

Arai and Fukuda had been conductors in the Tokyo area and, both being single, had often gone out drinking together after work. One night they had been drinking in the Shinjuku area when they got into a fight with three office workers. They had both boxed in high school and easily beat their opponents, and if that had been all there was to it nothing more would have happened. They would probably have had to pay for the office workers' medical costs and that would have been the end of it, but unfortunately, they had taken one of their opponents' wallets. They had not really meant anything by it, they had been very drunk at the time, but the result was that they were arrested for robbery and sentenced to two months in prison, suspended for one year. This meant that they were still on probation.

The last man on the list, Kubota, had joined J.N.R. straight from high school and had worked as a mechanic for twelve years. He was very highly thought of and had won several awards for diligence, but for some reason he had turned to drugs. It had probably started with some amphetamines to help him work nights, but it ended with his being dismissed from his job.

6

Kitano still did not know whether these four men were really part of the gang or not, but if Takano had decided that he needed some ex-railwaymen in his gang, it would have been very easy for him to have found out about these from all the press coverage they had received. They would also have been known by the crew on the Mystery Train and could very easily have tried to get Uehara to join them in their scheme. Kitano went through the files and found photographs and personal histories of all four men and took these with him to police headquarters.

"Much as I hate to say it, I think it might be worth your while to check on these four men," he said as he gave Totsugawa the envelope containing all the information.

"I know how you must feel," Totsugawa said, knowing that if there was a suspicion of a policeman having been involved, he would not like to admit it either.

He wrote the four names on the blackboard together with Takano's and Shiraishi's. The note they had found in Ishiyama's apartment hinted that there were eight people in the gang, and if they were to add Ishiyama to the others, it would still only add up to seven.

"Do you think this is the whole gang?"

"I don't know; what do you think?"

Totsugawa guessed that Takano was probably the mastermind behind the operation, and he would have gathered together only those people he considered necessary for the plan to succeed. Shiraishi would have been necessary to supply the buses to move the hostages from the station to the school, and the railwaymen would have been needed for their skills. He would have found out about them from the press. They would have become so hardened by the way they had been treated that it probably would not have taken much to persuade them to join in the plan.

"Who else would be necessary?" Totsugawa asked, looking at the blackboard. However, he was not asking Kitano so much as himself. Who else would be necessary to hijack a train and collect the ransom for the hostages?

"I think these six people would have been ample to hijack the train and kidnap the passengers," Kitano said. "They controlled the hostages with dynamite, so they would not need many people."

"But that means they needed someone who knew how to

handle explosives. You use a lot of dynamite on the railways, don't you?"

"Yes, we use it in construction, especially the construction of tunnels and the like, but our security is excellent."

"There were twelve sticks of dynamite used in the school and they had fuses, too. Could you check and make sure that there is no dynamite missing from any of the railway sites? If there is, we must check to see who had access to it and where they are now."

"I will get on it straight away," Kitano said and hurried back to the J.N.R. office.

Totsugawa looked at his watch impatiently. It was already five o'clock. Where were the kidnappers now? Were the three hostages and five railwaymen safe? He looked irritably at the three telephones on his desk. He had not heard a thing from Ogawa, who had gone to the house in Karasuyama, or from Kamei, who had gone to the factory in Mitaka.

What can they be doing? he thought.

The more time passed, the more irritable he became. The longer they took in tracing the kidnappers, the greater the likelihood that they would get away. They could already have escaped overseas, and if they managed to get away with all the ransom money, it would mean that the police had been beaten at every turn.

THE
RADAR SCREEN

1

Kitano invited seven of the released hostages over to the J.N.R. headquarters to answer some questions. They were all sensible people who seemed to be very observant, and among them was Kenichi Tsuyama, the reporter from the travel magazine *Ryoso*.

Kitano began by showing them photographs of the staff of the Mystery Train and asked if they had seen them when they were being held hostage. They all replied in the negative and he realized that they must have been kept somewhere else.

"Didn't you think it strange when the train stopped at Shin Tarui Station and you were all told to get into the coaches they had waiting?"

Tsuyama gave a wry grin.

"The detective on the bullet train asked us the same thing, but I am afraid that we didn't. You see, we were all fooled by the fact that it was a Mystery Train, no matter what happened, we would all have been willing to go along with it as we thought that it was part of the plan. On top of that, Shin Tarui Station is a very interesting place for railway freaks, they had a welcome arch out

205

over the exit and we were led away by uniformed conductors, so nobody thought there was anything amiss. I work for a travel magazine and I thought it was a little strange that they wanted us to go with them in coaches, so I left that note in my card holder, but even I was not completely aware of any danger."

"You did not see these five men on the bus?" Kitano asked, showing them the pictures of the train's crew.

"I don't think so," Tsuyama replied and the other six people nodded.

This meant that the crew of the train must have already been under the gang's control when the train pulled into the station. The gang must have taken over the train during the night when all the passengers were sleeping, and then kept them in the locomotive or generator car until the passengers had been taken away.

"What happened when you got to the school building?"

A girl of about twenty-six laughed and took up the story.

"They had another arch over the door with the words 'Welcome Mystery Train' written on it, so we didn't give it a second thought and went straight up to the fifth and sixth floors where they had laid out a breakfast of sandwiches and soda for us."

"Is that what they always gave you to eat? Soda and sandwiches?"

"No, from the second day, it was biscuits and soda," said a man of about fifty.

"I see, it would be easy for them to put in a stock of biscuits without anyone becoming suspicious."

"When we were eating our breakfast that first day, they suddenly closed all the doors and told us that we were prisoners."

"Did you soon grasp the situation?"

"No," replied a man in his forties who had said that his hobby was model railways. "At first we thought it was a joke, but when they put padlocks on the doors and produced shotguns, we were forced to take them seriously."

"You say they had guns?"

"Yes, they had two shotguns, but I was more worried about the dynamite."

"Were you able to pick up anything from their conversations? About the ransom money or how they hoped to escape afterward?"

"No, they did not talk much," one of them replied.

"They never called each other by name either," said another. "I think they were scared that we would learn their identities."

Much as he hated to, Kitano's next job was to show the former hostages the photos of the four ex-railwaymen who had been added to the list of suspects.

They all looked at the photos carefully and were soon able to pick out the ex-driver, Kajima, and the ex-conductor, Arai. They said that they thought the other two could have been there, too, but they were not sure.

Kitano realized that no matter how painful it may be for him, he had to admit that there was now no doubt that there were ex-railwaymen in the gang, and he hated to think what the press would have to say about that.

2

Kitano thanked them for their help and let them go home. No sooner had he done so than he had a call from the man in charge of the work to electrify the San-in line to tell him that a large amount of explosives had been stolen from there.

"Can you tell me exactly how much has disappeared?"

"It is over ten sticks, but I cannot say exactly. I don't think it is as many as twenty though."

"Can you give me some kind of idea of when it was stolen?"

"We are very busy here and cannot check on it every day, you know, but I think it was probably some time in the last two weeks."

"Do you know who stole it?"

"One of the companies that we are employing to do some of the work, K Construction, told me that an employee of their's disappeared recently without giving a reason."

"What is his name?"

"Why, Isamu Yamazaki, twenty-nine. He dropped out of university where he was studying engineering and has worked at various construction companies since then. He has been with K Construction since March last year and is single."

"What kind of person is he?"

"According to his colleagues he did not talk much, did not drink, and did not gamble. None of them really knew what he was thinking about."

"What were his hobbies?"

"He liked travel and used to go on trips for his holidays."

"You don't know if he was a member of a travel club called Nennikai, do you?"

"I don't know about that, all I know is that he liked to travel."

"What were his specialities? Did he knew how to use dynamite?"

"I should think so, that was his job. He also had a truck license, and I heard that he used to work as a driver sometimes."

If he drove a truck, he could just as easily have driven one of the buses from Shin Tarui Station. He had probably met Takano through the Nennikai club and when Takano realized that he would need someone who could handle dynamite, he could have approached him and offered him a share of the ransom.

"If you have a picture of the man, I would be grateful if you could get it to me as soon as possible," he said and hung up.

3

It was at about this time that Kamei and Sakurai arrived at the Tajima Mitaka factory. It was a huge affair, about half a mile from Mitaka Station with a sign outside saying, "Tajima Heavy Industries, Aircraft Division."

Dealing as it did in the latest technology, there was a strict guard on the gate, and if they had not had their police I.D.s, they would probably have gone no farther.

"We would like to speak to Mr. Taichiro Hayashi, please," Kamei said.

One of the guards picked up a telephone and made a call.

"I am afraid that Mr. Hayashi is not on the premises at the moment."

"Where is he?"

"I am afraid that I do not know, sir."

"What do you mean 'you don't know'? Let me see his assistant then."

"That would be Mr. Sano, the assistant manager."

The guard made another call, and this time he smiled when he looked up.

"Mr. Sano says that he can see you; his office is on the second floor of that building down there on the right."

The factory consisted of three huge buildings with a runway behind. The building that the guard pointed to was a small one to one side of the main factory.

They went up to the second floor and found the assistant manager's office next to the manager's. They knocked on the door and were shown in by a shortish man in his mid-forties.

"What do the police want with me?" he asked and indicated that they should take a seat.

"Actually, we wanted to discuss something with Mr. Hayashi, but we were told that he was out."

"Yes."

"Where has he gone? Will he be coming back today?"

"No, I am afraid not. He has gone to Taiwan."

"Taiwan? What for?"

"We make this airplane here," he said, pointing to a photograph on the wall. It showed a very graceful, twin-engine, executive jet with a long fuselage. "The engines are made in America, but it has the capacity to carry twelve people and it has a long range, so it is very popular in lots of countries around the world."

"Has Mr. Hayashi gone to Taiwan to try and promote sales over there?"

"No, a Taiwanese company has already ordered two of them, one of them was delivered six months ago. Mr. Hayashi has gone to hand over the second one."

"What exactly will he do over there?"

"Well, he and seven experts from our company will be leaving from Narita in a few moments to take the plane to Taiwan and hand it over personally. They will be coming back on a China Airlines flight tomorrow."

"I take it that the seven people will all have their own passports?"

"Of course, they cannot very well go out of the country without them, can they?" Sano said with a laugh.

"Have all seven of them already left the factory?"

"Yes, they will all be going together."

"What kind of people are they? I take it that Mr. Hayashi is the top man in this factory . . ."

"They are all people who were involved in the construction of the plane. There have been several minor changes in design since we built the first model and they have gone over to explain them to the pilots and mechanics who will be using it."

"What time will the plane be leaving?"

Sano looked up at the clock on the wall.

"In two or three minutes."

"Two or three minutes!"

Kamei and Sakurai looked at each other in despair; they finally realized how the gang hoped to escape, but they might be too late to do anything about it. They had obviously known that the plane was due to be delivered that day and that it would be carrying eight passengers, all of whom would have passports. They also knew that Hayashi's daughter was on the Mystery Train and they had kidnapped her to force Hayashi to give them his colleagues' passports and fly them to Taiwan.

"Do the seven people include the pilot?"

"No. The pilot and co-pilot are not employed by us full time, they are veteran pilots who we employ whenever we need to deliver a plane."

"So that means that there are nine people on the plane altogether?"

"Yes, that is correct."

"What is the number of the plane?"

"JAF two thousand."

"May I borrow the telephone, please?" Kamei picked up the phone and called Narita Airport. "Hello, is that Narita Airport? A plane called JAF two thousand is due to take off from there shortly and I wondered if it had left yet."

"It left two minutes ago."

"Damn!" Kamei shouted in despair.

4

At around the same time Detective Ogawa arrived at the pilot's house in Karasuyama. No matter how long he rang the front door bell, there was no answer, and so he had no choice but to find a phone and report in.

"There doesn't seem to be anyone at home, so what should I do? I have no warrant so I cannot very well force my way in."

"It doesn't matter, you can come back," Totsugawa replied.

"Are you sure?"

"Yes, I have just heard from Kamei and I think we can be pretty sure that Takatoshi Nakao is presently piloting a plane to Taiwan for Tajima Industries. That is why they had taken his daughter as a hostage."

He told them everything that he had learned from Kamei.

"I think we can be fairly sure that he is the pilot that was hired by Tajima."

"Has the plane already taken off?"

"Yes, but don't worry, it is still on the radar screens, all we have to do is call the airport and have them order it back."

"Okay, well, I will come straight back."

Totsugawa put the phone down and turned to Honda.

"I still don't understand it though," he said, looking worried.

"What?"

"What they hoped to do."

"I thought it was rather obvious. Not only have they managed to find a plane to fly them to Taiwan, but they also managed to get their hands on some passports. As it is a new plane that is being delivered to Taiwan, customs will not bother to check it very carefully. They would never guess that there is over a billion yen on board. When they get to Taiwan, they will hand over the plane, split up the money, and then all go their own ways. They have got Hayashi's daughter and the daughter of the pilot, Nakao, as hostages so they don't have to worry about them tipping off the police, and they will be able to use Japanese money quite easily in Taiwan, or they could go on to the Philippines or somewhere to live."

"But even though they slipped past us at the airport, we know where they are and where they are headed; all we have to do is get in touch with the police at the Taipei airport in Taiwan and have them arrested when they land."

"Yes, but only because we were lucky. How long would you say it takes to fly to Taiwan? About four hours?"

"Yes, four or five hours."

"Well, if we had been about five hours longer in working out what they planned, it would have been too late. I don't think they expected us to get on to them so quickly. Doing it this way means that they could escape abroad even though two of them don't have passports."

"That may be true, but I can't understand why they would be willing to risk everything on us taking longer to find them than we did. Up until now their plans have been flawless—they managed to hijack a train and then get the money without us being able to do a thing about it—but when it came to their escape, they were almost sloppy in their planning."

"You worry to much. We have got the plane on the radar and all we have to do now is to contact Interpol and have them arrested when they land," Honda said happily.

5

The radar room at air traffic control had very dim lighting so the technicians could see the screens easily. Narita had the latest type of radar installed, it could track planes for approximately two hundred miles and next to each blip on the screen was a notation giving the call numbers of the plane.

One of the controllers, Suzuki, was sitting in front of the screen watching the orange dot with its dim tail marked JAF 2000. The dot represented the position of the aircraft and the tail showed the direction it was moving. Even though it was moving at over three hundred and fifty miles per hour, it hardly seemed to move on the screen. It was flying at fifteen thousand feet and would shortly be moving out over Sagami Bay.

"Come in please, Juliet Alpha Foxtrot two thousand, come in. You are to return to Narita immediately, over . . . Do you read me Juliet Alpha Foxtrot two thousand, please return to Narita immediately."

The air traffic controller was calling out to the plane, but it was in vain, he got no reply. He had heard from the police that there was a gang of kidnappers on board and he guessed that the pilot was being prevented from answering his calls. However, the plane could not escape from the radar.

The blip on the screen looked like a firefly struggling to escape from a round cage.

"I will get in touch with the Self-Defense Force," the chief controller said. "If they take off from Hamamatsu they should be able to meet JAF two thousand over Sagami Bay."

He rang the base and, almost immediately, two Phantoms took off and the base controller came on the line asking for a fix on the target plane. The call was transferred to Suzuki, who was watching the plane on the screen and his directions would be transmitted directly to the pilots of the two Phantoms. He had to be accurate; the Phantoms were fitted with radar, but they did not know which of the blips on their screens was their target. Finding a particular plane in the sky was not the easiest of tasks. Suzuki did not take his eyes off the screen.

"Juliet Alpha Foxtrot two thousand is presently flying at an altitude of fifteen thousand feet at a speed of three hundred and two knots and is presently heading southwest at . . . What!"

In all the seven years he had been employed as a controller, he had never seen anything like it.

"Hello, Narita, what is the plane's position, please?"

"Juliet Alpha Foxtrot two thousand has just disappeared."

"Hello, Narita, could you repeat that, please?"

"It just disappeared right off the screen!"

"What the hell are you talking about? Look at your screen!" the chief controller shouted and hurried down to Suzuki's booth.

"I am looking, sir," Suzuki said, almost in tears. "The blip and label have disappeared from the screen."

"You are right," the chief controller said, looking over his shoulder. "Is the equipment malfunctioning?"

"No, all the other planes are still present, sir."

"You mean just JAF two thousand has disappeared?"

"Yes, sir. I cannot understand it unless JAF two thousand has crashed . . ."

"Are you sure that it did not just drop its altitude in order to escape our radar?"

"That is impossible, sir."

"Why?"

"JAF two thousand was flying at fifteen thousand feet; if it wanted to avoid our radar, it would have to drop to at least one thousand feet. But that plane is not aerobatic, it would not be able to lose altitude quickly enough to disappear from the screen like that without crashing."

"So you mean that something happened and it crashed?"

"There is no other explanation."

6

When they heard that JAF two thousand had disappeared from the radar, the two Phantoms had no option but to return to base.

Honda and Totsugawa also did not know quite how to take the news.

"Are you quite sure that the plane disappeared from the screen?" Totsugawa asked.

"Yes, there is no mistake about it," the chief controller answered. "It disappeared quite suddenly and we think it must have blown up in midair."

"Was the controller who saw this on the screen Hideo Hoshino?" Totsugawa asked, thinking that the gang may have kidnapped Hoshino's daughter in order to force him to pretend that the plane had disappeared when really nothing had happened at all. This, however, was not the case.

"No, the controller was Kenichi Suzuki and I also looked at the screen. There is no mistake, JAF two thousand disappeared from the screen."

"Where is Hideo Hoshino at the moment?"

"I think he is taking a break."

"I see . . ."

"We are treating it as an accident and have called out the coast guard to search the area for wreckage."

Totsugawa asked where the plane had disappeared and then hung up. He picked up an atlas of Japan and looked for the position on the map.

"He says that he thinks it blew up in midair and crashed into the sea," he told Honda.

"If they can manage to come up with any wreckage, there will be no point in contacting the police in Taiwan. I never thought the case would end like this."

Honda looked at the map and Totsugawa drew a red circle on it with a felt-tip pen to mark the spot where it was thought the plane had crashed.

"I suppose this means that the money has disappeared into the sea together with the gang."

"Yes, but it doesn't feel right. It isn't the way I visualized the case ending."

"If they find some wreckage, I suppose we will have to accept the fact that they are now beyond the law. It is a shame, I was looking forward to arresting this lot," Totsugawa said.

They could do nothing else about the gang now until they heard the results of the search, but there were still the eight hostages to look for. Totsugawa was quite optimistic about finding them alive because, contrary to his earlier fears, the gang did not seem to be very bloodthirsty after all. So far three hundred and ninety-seven of the hostages had been released without an injury among them, and although the gang had killed the conductor and the man from the travel club, it apparently had been because they had refused to cooperate. As long as the eight remaining hostages had not done anything stupid, there was no reason to think anything would happen to them. As far as he knew, all the kidnappers had been on the plane when it disappeared, so there would be no one guarding the hostages. They were probably locked up somewhere like the people at the school in Shin Tarui were to ensure that they did not try to escape.

"Do you think the hostages are being kept in the west of the country?" Honda asked.

"Yes, I think it is likely. There would be no point in bringing them all the way up to Tokyo, would there?"

But where could they be imprisoned and had the gang really died in Sagami Bay?

THE
LIFE JACKET

1

News of the plane's disappearance was soon announced on television and radio. The police had purposely not suppressed the news as they were interested to see what reaction it would bring. They did not have to wait long; soon after the announcement was made on the radio Totsugawa received a phone call.

"There is something that I think I should tell you about flight JAF two thousand."

"My name is Totsugawa of the first investigation division, what would you like to tell me?"

The man seemed to be discussing it with someone else for a minute.

"I do not think I should talk about it over the telephone. Can I meet you?" he asked, his voice tense.

"Of course, would you like to come over here?"

"Yes, I will be right over."

"Excuse me, but could I have your name?"

"I'm sorry; it is Koike."

"Very well, we will be waiting for you, Mr. Koike."

The man arrived by taxi about thirty minutes later. He was

a smartly dressed man of about thirty and gave Totsugawa a business card that introduced him as being a member of the aircraft division at Tajima Heavy Industries. This was just what Totsugawa had been hoping for.

"I take it that you were one of the men who was supposed to have been on that plane today?"

"Yes, that is correct."

"Would you like to tell me about it?"

"As you seem to know, I am one of the seven members of our staff who were due to fly over to Taiwan on the JAF two thousand today, but this morning Mr. Hayashi called us all together and begged us for our passports. He told us that his daughter and the daughter of the pilot who always flies our planes had been kidnapped and that the people who had done it were demanding that they be flown to Taiwan."

"Did he mention how many there were in the gang?"

"Yes, he said that there were seven of them and that they wanted our passports and the passport of the co-pilot to use for themselves."

"Did you hand them over?"

Totsugawa did not really mean anything by the question, but Koike looked up sharply.

"No, of course not, we told him to go to the police and tell you all about it, but we knew how he felt about his only daughter and the pilot was the same, so we could not refuse him. Mr. Hayashi started the aircraft division at our company and taught us all we know; we could not ignore him when he needed us."

"Then what happened?"

"The kidnappers said that they would return the hostages after they had arrived in Taiwan. They promised that nothing would happen to Mr. Hayashi or the pilot, so we decided to wait until they came back before we went to the police. We handed over our passports and stayed out of sight since we were supposed to be on the plane, but you can imagine our shock when we heard that it had disappeared over the sea. Did the plane really crash?" Koike asked, looking up at Totsugawa with a pale face.

"Well, I am not very much of an expert about such things, but it would appear that it disappeared suddenly from the radar screens."

"I see," Koike said with a sigh. "Now I wish that we had come straight to you when we first heard about it, that way you could have stopped the plane from taking off and Mr. Hayashi would be all right."

"Did you see the kidnappers?"

"No, we didn't."

"Who did you give the passports to?"

"We believed Mr. Hayashi and gave all our passports to him."

2

The families of the pilot, Nakao, and Hayashi also got in touch with the police and told them that while they knew what was happening, they could not come forward as they were worried about what would happen to the hostages if they did.

The investigation team held a conference to discuss this turn in the case.

"The coast guard has already started an investigation of the area in which the plane was thought to have gone down," Totsugawa said.

"I never thought the case would end like this," Honda said with a disgruntled expression. "If it had just been the gang on board, we could have left things as they were, since it would seem that they were suitably punished, but as Mr. Hayashi and Mr. Nakao were also on board, not to mention the money, we must hope that something shows up."

"Is there anything we can do?"

"We will have to leave the search up to the coast guard, but we still have to find the hostages that weren't released. There are three passengers and five members of the train's crew, which makes eight people altogether. I think it would be safe to assume that they are being held somewhere in the west of the country."

"Do you think they may have been killed?"

"No, we managed to release the other three hundred and ninety-seven without any of them being hurt. I think it would be safe to say that the kidnappers do not mean to hurt this last eight either. They were due to arrive in Taiwan at about eight o'clock this evening, Japan time, so I think the hostages have been left some place where they will be found at about that time. I think, as in the last case, they will be locked somewhere without anyone to guard them."

"Can we be sure that there were seven people in the gang?"

"Yes, I think so, I have written their names on the blackboard over there," Totsugawa said.

Masashi Takano	ex-school proprietor
Takeshi Shiraishi	ex-owner of bus company
Taiichi Kajima	ex-train driver
Mikio Arai	ex-conductor
Tetsu Fukuda	ex-conductor
Ken Kubota	ex-mechanic
Isamu Yamazaki	explosives expert

Totsugawa had managed to obtain photographs of each of them and he gave copies of these to each of the investigators even though it seemed pointless now that they were all at the bottom of the sea somewhere in the wreckage of the plane.

"About the hostages' families," Honda said, "we have heard from the relatives of Hayashi and Nakao, but we have not heard anything from the family of the air traffic controller, Hoshino. Why do you think this is?"

"Unlike the other two, he was not due to fly on the plane, so his family did not have any reason to worry when they heard that the plane had disappeared."

"What is he doing now?"

"We learned from the air traffic control center that he left work at about midday, but he has yet to return home. I can only guess that he has gone to look for his son on his own."

"Why do you think the kidnappers wanted to take his son? I can understand them wanting to kidnap the daughters of the other two, as it would give them a ticket to Taiwan and freedom, but why an air traffic controller?"

"Maybe they wanted someone in the control tower on their side when they took off."

"But he worked in the control center, not the control tower at the airport," Honda pointed out.

Totsugawa couldn't answer him. When he first heard that the kidnappers had kept the son of an air traffic controller, he just vaguely felt that he would be useful for them to escape abroad, but when he thought about it logically, he realized that he could not understand what help he could be.

This question was left unsettled and they moved on to the next point on the agenda.

"Do you think we should start a public investigation now?" Honda asked.

3

If all of the kidnappers were on the business jet that crashed off the coast in Sagami Bay, it would be quite safe for the police to open a public investigation, but if one of them had remained to guard the hostages, it would be very dangerous for them to act rashly now.

"I don't think there is any chance that a member of the gang would have remained in the country," Totsugawa said.

"Why do you say that?" Honda asked.

"The leaders, Takano and Shiraishi, could have left the country as soon as they got their hands on the ransom—we still did not know who they were—but they chose to remain with the others until they could all get out together. We know that two of them were on probation, which meant that they could not get passports, and yet they waited until they could all leave, so I think it unlikely that one of them would have remained behind to guard the hostages for the others. If we had not realized how they intended to leave the country, there was a good chance that they would all have been free in Taiwan by eight o'clock tonight with passports to take them on to other countries if they wanted. So I don't see why one of them would take the risk of staying behind when he could have been with them."

Totsugawa was very confident, but it was up to his superiors to decide.

"Okay, I agree," Honda said. "I will recommend that we open a public investigation."

This marked the end of that day's conference.

Honda and Totsugawa went to see Chief Inspector Mikami and asked him to approve an open investigation, but he was not as willing as they had hoped. He had not taken an active role in the investigation and, as a result, his judgment was more politically biased than theirs.

"You tell me that there is no need to worry, but what would you do if the gang had left someone to guard the hostages after all? If we opened a public investigation, he might panic and kill the hostages before he tried to escape. Can you be one hundred percent sure that this will not happen?"

"No, sir, I cannot."

It was impossible to be one hundred percent sure about anything in the inquiry, it was the same in a murder investigation, but he felt that it should be up to the man in the field to decide what form the investigation should take.

"I will take full responsibility, sir," Honda said.

"That is very easy for you to say, but should something go wrong, I will be held ultimately responsible," Mikami replied irritably.

"But if we delay any longer and the hostages suffer as a result, surely you will have to take the responsibility for that, too," Honda said.

Mikami looked even more irritable than before.

"So the press is going to blame me whether we go public or not."

"The press only judges a case on results. I think we stand a better chance of getting good results if we go public. The hostages have been held for three days now, and I think it is very important that we get them out as soon as possible. I also think it is likely that they are being held in the west of the country, and the only way we are going to find them quickly is to go public without delay."

Honda was usually a very quiet man who did not try to force his opinion on other people like this, and eventually Mikami was forced to agree to go public.

4

The waters of Sagami Bay sparkled brilliantly in the afternoon sun, making it hard to see from the coast guard's YS11 that circled slowly over the area where flight JAF 2000 was thought to have gone down. Down below there were two coast guard cutters also helping in the search; the sky above was also filled with small planes belonging to various newspaper and television companies. When the YS11 had first arrived on the scene, it had been alone in its search, but suddenly it was joined by a multitude of light aircraft, and this was because the police had finally gone public with their investigation.

Mikami had held a press conference at around six o'clock and asked for assistance in locating the eight hostages. At the same time, he told them that seven members of the gang had tried to escape to Taiwan in an executive jet belonging to Tajima Heavy Industries, but that the plane had disappeared from the radar over Sagami Bay.

The result was that all the papers present immediately sent aircraft out to look for signs of the wreckage and prepared headlines such as, "One Billion Yen Disappears into the Sea Together with Kidnappers!"

The crew on the coast guard cutter *Sandpiper* looked up in disgust at the aircraft circling above as they scanned the waters for any sign of wreckage. Their sister ship, *Plover*, had also had no luck, but they would keep looking for as long as the light held.

The two ships had hurried to the site as soon as they heard what had happened. They had been told only that a twin-engine executive jet had disappeared from the radar, but they had no idea why. It could have gone into a dive and hit the water, or it could have exploded in midair. In the first case, there was very little chance of finding any wreckage, but if it had exploded, there should be a lot of wreckage scattered over the whole area. Of course, the pilot could have succeeded in making a crash landing on the sea, and in that case there was a good chance of finding survivors.

They had been searching for about an hour without any success when one of the lookouts on the *Sandpiper* called out: "Object to starboard!"

The skipper picked up his binoculars and looked over to the right. There, floating on the black water, was an orange object. He felt a shock of excitement run through him and ordered both engines stopped. The boat glided past the object before it could come to a halt and although the crew tried to catch it with boathooks, they could not reach it, so a boat was lowered to go pick it up.

5

The object turned out to be an aircraft's life jacket and it had the words "Tajima Heavy Industries" written on the top.

The captain of the ship knew that the missing plane had

belonged to Tajima Heavy Industries, so he ordered the mate to contact their base with the number of the life jacket in order to check which plane it had belonged to.

They continued their search while they were waiting, and thirty minutes later they learned that it had indeed been one of the life jackets on board flight JAF 2000. The fact that a life jacket had been found at all would seem to indicate that the people on board had been able to get off the plane after it crashed or had been thrown out. The sea was calm and, since it was summer, quite warm, so there was a fair chance that the plane's passengers could still be alive. The coast guard stepped up their search. About twenty-five minutes later the *Plover* found another life jacket, and after checking with Tokyo, it was confirmed that this, too, was from the missing plane. They did not know what had happened to the plane, but it was certain that it went down in this area.

The water here was about three hundred fathoms deep and there was very little likelihood of the plane itself ever coming to light.

They heard on the radio that the plane had been carrying a gang that had kidnapped four hundred passengers on the Mystery Train and received one billion yen in ransom. They were amazed at the size of the ransom, and they felt that it was only fair that the gang had been unable to enjoy the money. They were very sorry for the two men who had been forced to go on the plane with them, the pilot and the man from Tajima Heavy Industries, and they hoped that they could at least find these two. They put all their energies into the search, but two hours passed and still all they had to show for their efforts were the two life jackets. Everything else from the plane had disappeared without a trace.

6

All the papers brought out special editions with full reports of the case and photographs of the missing hostages. The television covered the story in detail on the news and even interrupted its scheduled programs with updates.

Totsugawa and Kamei were watching the reports on the television when the news came in that the two life jackets belonging to flight JAF 2000 had been found in Sagami Bay.

"This means that there was no mistake, the plane did crash," Kamei said disappointedly.

Totsugawa took out the map where he had marked the spot that the plane disappeared and they looked at it in silence. The water at that point was very deep and they could never bring the plane back up to the surface, even if they could locate it. They guessed that the passengers and pilot must have been trapped in the plane when it went down, and so now they would never have the satisfaction of arresting the gang.

"It is a pity, isn't it?" Totsugawa said.

The whole police force was now involved in a nationwide search for the missing hostages, but they still did not have any leads. They had found the passengers of the Mystery Train in a school belonging to Takano, but, unfortunately, he did not have any other schools in that part of the country.

"This time there are only eight people, so they could be almost anywhere."

"That is true, but they could not very well keep them in an apartment somewhere; the neighbors would become suspicious if they made any noise," Totsugawa said, thinking. He felt, somehow, that the gang was much more likely to have kept them in a quiet place in the country where nobody was likely to find them. "Don't you think they would be more likely to hide them in a holiday villa in the mountains somewhere?"

"You mean use someone else's without their knowing? But it is midsummer now; everyone who owns a villa is likely to be using it themselves."

"Yes, that is true, I suppose."

"Did Takano or Shiraishi own a villa?"

"Let's check it out."

This, however, turned out to be another blind alley. Takano had bought a villa while he was doing well, but it was not in the west of the country, it had been on Oahu Island in Hawaii. It had been a huge place with plenty of land and it would appear that he had intended to use it as a summer camp, but it had passed out of his hands when he began having financial difficulties. Shiraishi had also owned a villa in a place called Shirahama, but he had lost that when he went bankrupt, and it now belonged to a company that kept it for its employees to use.

"Well, it was a good idea, anyway," Totsugawa said.

But where else could eight people be held captive without anyone knowing? It was the summer holidays so the schools would all be empty, but as Totsugawa had found out himself, the staff members took turns staying there guarding the premises so nobody could use one without it being noticed.

"We will just have to wait for someone to tip us off," Totsugawa said. After all, that was the reason why they had decided to make the investigation public in the first place.

He reached for the phone and dialed Hoshino's number.

7

Hoshino's wife answered the phone and when Totsugawa told her who he was, she sounded very worried.

"Is my son all right? Can you be sure that they won't kill him now that you have put the story on the television?"

"Of course he is all right; we would not have gone public if we thought there was the slightest chance of his coming to any harm. I am sure that we will find him soon, so please don't worry," Totsugawa said reassuringly. "By the way, have you heard from your husband yet?"

"No, I have not heard a word. I wish he would call though."

"Do you have any idea where he might be?"

"He dotes on his son, so I guess he is out somewhere looking for him."

"I see. If you hear from him, please tell him to get in touch with the police straight away?" Totsugawa said and put the phone down.

Kamei came over to him.

"Are you worried about him?"

"Yes, I am a little. He knows that the investigation has gone public and that the airplane the gang were escaping in crashed into the sea, so why doesn't he come forward? He hasn't even contacted his wife, but why?"

"Didn't you just say that you thought he was out looking for his son?" Kamei said, surprised.

"Only because I could not think of anything else."

"Do you still think that is what he is doing?"

"Well, I can understand why he might feel that he cannot trust us to find his son and would not be able to rest until he had found him himself, but how would he go about doing it?"

"That is true, we don't know ourselves, we can only guess that he is in the west of the country somewhere. Hoshino can't know any more than we do, and even if he did, surely he would come to us for help."

"He cannot just be walking around blindly looking for him though; I think there is something suspicious about his behavior."

"You don't think he is one of the gang, do you?"

"One of the gang?" Totsugawa repeated in surprise.

"Yes, he could have been a member of the gang and planted a bomb on the plane in order to destroy all the evidence. He worked at the air traffic control center, so he could have had plenty of opportunity to plant the bomb and now he is just waiting to make sure that we are not on to him. He could have hidden his son with the other hostages so that he could pretend to be one of the victims and we would never suspect him."

"It is an interesting theory, but I am afraid that I can't go along with it."

"Then why do you think he hasn't shown up yet?"

"I don't know, but I feel that it could be very important to this case. I think we should have the television put out a message for him to come forward straight away."

THE
SOUTHERN SKY

1

Totsugawa asked the television companies to appeal to Hoshino to contact the police, and all stations carried the message after the news of the case. He also had the radio stations carry the appeal in case Hoshino was walking around looking for his son with nothing but a transister radio to listen to. However, they did not hear anything from him.

"There is definitely something strange about this," Totsugawa said.

"Maybe Hoshino is walking around somewhere and has not listened to the radio or television," Kamei suggested, but Totsugawa shook his head.

"I don't think that is the way a man whose son has been kidnapped would behave. I don't know what his part in the escape was, but I think we must assume that he did whatever it was he was told to do, and if that is the case, you would think that he would telephone his wife to see if their son had been released and watch the television for any news."

"That is true," Kamei said, nodding. "The fact that he has

233

not done so must either mean that he is in league with the kidnappers or he is being restrained by them."

"I think we can forget about him being a member of the gang, which means that the gang must be restraining him somehow. The television and radio are full of the news of the plane crash and the disappearance of the passengers, and the newspapers have all brought out special editions, so it is very unlikely that he has not heard about it, and yet he still continues to do what he has been told. The families of the pilot and Mr. Hayashi got in touch as soon as they heard the news, and so did the staff from Tajima Heavy Industries. Hoshino is the only one who has yet to get in touch with us, and I cannot understand why."

"Where on earth could he be?"

"I think there are two possibilities."

"What are they?"

"One is that he knows the gang is still alive and is too scared to come forward."

"Just a minute!" Kamei exclaimed, looking at Totsugawa in surprise. "We know for a fact that the plane carrying the gang crashed on its way to Taiwan."

"It has not been proved yet."

"But two life jackets were found in the sea and it disappeared suddenly from the radar screen. That is proof enough for the coast guard to say unofficially that they believe it crashed."

"The life jackets could have been thrown from the plane when it was flying low. We were told that the pilot's side window can be opened."

"Why? to make us think they had crashed?"

"Exactly."

"But how do you explain the fact that the plane disappeared suddenly from the radar screen? It would be impossible for a plane of that type to go into a steep dive from fifteen thousand feet to an altitude where it would be able to escape the radar without it breaking up, and if it descended more gently, its maneuvers would have been picked up by the radar."

"That is true, but I can't help but feel suspicious that Hoshino worked in the same radar room. It might be possible for someone to make an aircraft disappear from the radar, and that may be what he did."

"It sounds a bit like magic to me."

"That is only because we are both amateurs when it comes to this kind of thing. I want you to get over to the airport and check it out."

"Right away."

"The second thing is, if he did know that the plane had crashed but has still not come forward, the question is, as you said just now, where is he?"

"What do you mean?"

"It is possible that he knows where his son is being held and has gone to rescue him. He could have been in such a hurry that he forgot all about contacting us."

"But why would the gang only tell him and not the other people, too? Also, if he knew where his son was being held, surely he would have gone to find him this morning instead of waiting at the air traffic control center until lunchtime."

"I cannot even begin to answer those questions, the mere fact that he has not come forward is a mystery and I don't think it can be explained logically any other way."

"So what shall we do?"

"Well, I would like you to get on down to the air traffic control center and check up on the first theory while I arrange for a nationwide search for Hoshino. I don't think he is connected with the gang directly, but I do think he holds the key to the mystery."

2

At a little after eight o'clock a solitary man wearing sun-glasses changed from the Tokaido line to the Tarumi line. The Tarumi line is a small branch line that runs fifteen miles between Ogaki and Minokomi and the two-car train only makes an average of eleven round-trips a day, though it makes thirteen trips on Saturdays and only ten on Sundays.

Outside, it was already dark, but there was a moon, and the man sat looking out of the window. At first the train ran parallel to the Tokaido line, but then it veered northward toward the mountains.

It came to the first station that was unmanned and nobody got on or off. Of the ten stations on the line, only one of them is manned.

The man took a note out of his pocket and read it; it said Kochibora Station. Outside, the fields gave way to low moun-tains and there was little sign of life. The train arrived at Kochibora Station at eight fifty-seven and the man got off.

This station was also unmanned, but an elderly couple who looked like locals also got off at this station.

"Excuse me," the man said, approaching them.

"What is it?"

"Do you know if there is a water tower near here?"

"Water tower?"

"Yes, you know, a water tower that they used to use for filling the boilers on steam trains."

"Do you think he means that thing down there?" the woman asked, nodding down the tracks.

"Now that you mention it, there is a concrete tower down there, but it isn't used anymore."

"You mean that it is farther along the line?"

"Yes, it is about halfway between here and Tanigumiguchi Station."

"How long will it take to walk?"

"I don't know, it is about half a mile, I suppose."

The man thanked them and set off down the tracks in the direction that the train disappeared. The night had deepened, but the moon was bright enough for him to see by. He walked for about five minutes and, sure enough, he came to a concrete tower just as the couple had said. It was a round tower about twenty feet high, and it would appear that it had not been used for a long time as its walls were covered in creepers.

The Tarumi line had been completed in 1958, and although at that time electric locomotives were already in use in Japan, they were not considered to be reliable enough for regular work, and a new steam locomotive called the C63 had been designed to be used on the unelectrified lines. The C63, however, never got beyond the drawing board—diesel locomotives were adopted in its place—but it would appear that the water tower had been constructed with it in mind.

The tower itself had very thick concrete walls to enable it to withstand the vast pressure of the water it had been designed to hold; at the base there was a small steel door to enable men to get inside to repair it should it become damaged. The door, however, had been recently concreted over and would not open.

The man stood in front of the tower.

"Eiji! Hey, Eiji!" the man shouted, his voice echoing in the still night, but there was no reply. He took off his shoe and hit the door with the heel, but it only made a dull noise against the concrete and there was no answering sound.

"Eiji! Are you in there? Answer me!"

No matter how loud he shouted, the sound did not appear to get through the thick walls and there was no response. He sat down on the ground in front of the tower in exhaustion. He knew that he would have to get help, but there were no houses nearby and he did not know what to do.

At that moment, he heard the sound of a train approaching;

it was the same train that he had arrived on. It had gone on to the end of the line and was now making its way back to Ogaki.

The man took off his suit jacket and stood in the middle of the tracks waving at it furiously.

3

The train squealed to a halt and the driver opened his window.

"What the hell are you doing, standing there like that!" he shouted.

"You've got to help me," the man said in a hoarse voice.

"Why? What has happened?"

"My name is Hideo Hoshino; I am sure that they must be talking about me on the news by now."

"Now that you mention it, I do seem to remember seeing your face on the TV," the driver said, shining a torch in his face. "They said that your son had been kidnapped."

"That is why I need your help; he is in that water tower."

"In there?"

"Yes, there is a door at the base, but it has been cemented over and it will not budge."

"In that case, you will need the police to help you. You wait here and I will hurry down the line to Minomotosu and get in touch with them for you."

"Thank you very much," Hoshino said in relief.

4

Kamei sat in the radar room at the air traffic control center and looked around at the controllers peering tensely into their large screens while he talked to the man in charge.

"What is that thing like a typewriter that they have next to the screen," he asked.

"That? Oh, that is a computer keyboard," the chief controller answered.

"What do you use a computer for?"

"Well, in the old days the radar would only show the planes as dots on the screen, and we had to check out each one to see what they were. This was all right when there were only a few planes in the area, but when the airport was crowded, it meant that we had a screen full of dots to try and follow and it became quite confusing. Now we use a computer to sort things out."

"In what way?"

"Well, we input the data on all arrivals and departures at the airport. For instance, if a controller wanted to know where a certain plane that had left the airport twenty minutes ago was now, all he had to do would be to type in the code for that aircraft and the blip corresponding to the plane would appear on the screen with a label giving its flight number next to it."

"I see," Kamei said, nodding. "And would it be possible to tamper with the computer so that a plane on the screen would seem to disappear suddenly?"

"Yes, it would be quite possible," the chief controller replied.

"Are you sure about that?"

"Yes, I think it was at Kennedy Airport, but once an Aeroflot plane was approaching the runway and had just started its final descent when it suddenly disappeared from the radar. Everyone assumed that it had crashed on landing and there was a terrible panic."

"What happened?"

"It turned out that one of the controllers had a real antipathy toward the Soviets and he had doctored the radar to make it look as if it had crashed."

5

Kamei returned from Narita and made his report.

"Well, now, I think we know what Hoshino's role in all this was. He fixed the radar to make it look as if flight JAF two thousand crashed over Sagami Bay. Apparently it would be quite simple for someone like him to program the computer to make that happen, but we cannot prove anything."

"I see, so that was why they took his son hostage."

"Yes, he knew the kidnappers were still alive, that is why he did not come forward."

"That means that they landed in Taipei some time ago," Totsugawa said irritably.

They had intended to telephone the Taiwan police and have them hold the passengers when the plane arrived, but when they heard that it had crashed into the sea it no longer seemed necessary.

"I will get someone at the top to call the Taiwan police," Totsugawa said and hurried through to Honda's office.

"I will ask the chief inspector to get on it straight away, but don't we know where Hoshino is yet?" Honda asked.

"No, I am afraid not. I think the gang must have told him what to do after he had tinkered with the radar and that he is still acting on their instructions."

"But isn't that a bit strange? I am sure he would not have doctored the radar like that for a vague promise to release his son. I think they must have given him definite information about where he is being held."

"You are probably right."

"But surely if they had told him where he was, he would go and look for him straight away. Once he found him he would feel no compunction to do what the gang said. And if the boy wasn't there, he still would not do what he was told."

"Yes, the kidnappers must have somehow got in touch with him at about the time they arrived in Taiwan and he went straight to get his son instead of coming to us."

"How would they do that? Do you think they telephoned him from Taiwan?"

"No, he was not at home to take a call, and if they had had him wait for the call in a coffee bar somewhere there was a risk that he would have been recognized after we put out a call for him on the television. Anyway, if they were to call from Taiwan, there was always the chance that we would find out about it and that would tell us exactly where they had escaped to."

"So how do you think they did it?" Honda asked. At that moment they were interrupted by the phone on Honda's desk. "Excuse me a minute."

He sat in silence listening to the person on the other end of the line, his face suddenly growing brighter.

"On the Tarumi line, near Tanigumiguchi Station? Where does that leave from . . . ? Ogaki Station? You say that Hoshino is there as well as the hostages? Where? . . . In a water tower? Of course, one of my men will be right over."

"Have they found Hoshino and the hostages?"

"Yes, apparently. Could you pass me the atlas from that bookcase, please?"

He opened it to a map of central Japan.

"Tanigumiguchi is about fourteen miles from Ogaki Station and Ogaki is only about five miles from where the other hostages were held, so they were only about nineteen miles away all along," Totsugawa said.

6

It took them about an hour to break through the concrete on the door of the water tower, and when they finally got it open, one of the detectives shone his torch in to find all the hostages collapsed on the floor in exhaustion. They had been left a kerosene lamp, but that had long since gone out. They were taken to a hospital in three ambulances, Hoshino going in one of them with his son.

Although the tower had never actually been used to store water, it was very damp and the smell of mold mingled with the smell of the hostages' wastes, making a nauseating stench. The pipe for filling the tower with water had also been blocked off with cement and there was no way for air to get in.

"If we had been a day late in finding them, they would probably have never made it," one of the detectives remarked with a sigh as he looked around the interior.

The Tarumi line was one of the local lines that was destined for oblivion for the sake of economy, and the water tower would disappear with it. Nobody ever passed that way, and if they did, no one would give it a second glance. No matter how loudly the hostages may have shouted when the trains passed outside, there was nobody to hear them. If they had not been discovered, they would have remained incarcerated there forever.

It was two in the morning when Totsugawa and Kamei arrived in Ogaki at the hospital where the hostages were recovering from their ordeal. They had taken the last bullet train as far as Shizuoka and then traveled the remainder of the way by taxi.

"There is nothing wrong with any of them; they are just exhausted and need to rest for the moment. I think that after a good night's sleep, however, they will be able to answer your questions," the doctor in charge told them.

Totsugawa walked into the waiting room where he found Hoshino sitting on his own. He seemed very relieved now that his son had been rescued, and when he saw Totsugawa he bowed apologetically.

"I am very sorry for all the trouble I caused," he said.

"So it was you who tinkered with the computer at air traffic control?"

"You know about that?"

"Yes, but you had us fooled for a while, and not only us. Air traffic control, the air force, and the coast guard all believed that flight JAF two thousand had gone down in Sagami Bay, and as a result the kidnappers managed to get away."

"I am very sorry, but my son was being held hostage so I had no choice." Hoshino looked very haggard.

"Don't worry, no one is going to blame you for what you did, but we would like to know how you learned that your son was being held in the water tower."

"The man who told me to tamper with the radar said that if I did exactly as I was told, I would be able to find out where my son was at eight twenty-five last night, but that I was not to say anything to the police."

"Why eight twenty-five?"

"He told me that after I had fixed the computer, I was to go to Nagoya, where I would find a company outside the station called S Air Freight. He said that a package for a Hideo Tanaka would arrive there at eight twenty-five and that if I was to pick it up, it would contain directions to my son's whereabouts."

He took out a brown envelope and handed it to Totsugawa. Inside were a magazine and a single sheet of paper with the following message:

Your son is in a water tower next to the Tarumi line near Kochibora station.

7

"We checked the sender's address, but it was false," said a local policeman who was standing nearby.

"Did you check with S Air Freight?"

"Yes, they have got a national network of offices, and if a package is handed into their Tokyo branch by eleven in the morning, it should arrive at their Nagoya office at five twenty-five."

"Don't they deliver?"

"Yes, if they are requested to, but not until the following morning."

This meant that one of the members of the gang must have gone to the Tokyo office, handed in the package, and then gone on to meet his colleagues at the airport.

The hostages had recovered sufficiently by noon to talk to the police. The crew of the train had been taken straight to the water tower from the Mystery Train and kept there under guard until they were joined by the other three. After that the door had been cemented closed, but the gang told them that they would be rescued on the evening of the eleventh, and that they should wait quietly until then.

"It was just as they said, although if we had had to wait another day, some of us might not have made it. The child, in particular, was very weak," said Masato Nakamura, the driver of the Mystery Train.

They had all seen their captors and when Totsugawa showed them photographs of the suspects, they agreed that these were the ones responsible. The only problem was that it was too late, the kidnappers had managed to get away to Taiwan, and since they all had passports, where they would go from there was anybody's guess.

Totsugawa telephoned Honda at headquarters to report on everything and bring him up to date.

"The hostages are all fit and well and they positively identified the suspects for us. It is a shame that we could not have found out about them a bit earlier so we could have stopped them from getting away. I really wanted to catch this lot myself, and I would have done anything to have stopped them from slipping through our fingers like that."

"In that case, you can have the job of going out to Taiwan

to pick them up. I will let you choose who you want to take with you."

"You mean they were arrested in Taiwan?" Totsugawa asked in amazement.

"Yes, the Foreign Ministry got in touch with me a short while ago and told me that they were all arrested at the airport."

"But I thought we didn't bother to contact the police over there after we thought the plane had crashed."

"That is true."

"Did the immigration authorities there notice that their passports belonged to other people?"

"No, all nine of the people on the plane were arrested, including Hayashi and the pilot."

"What the . . . What were they arrested for?"

"Spying."

"Huh?"

"Well, from what I can gather, Taiwan officials found a copy of *The Thoughts of Chairman Mao* under one of the seats in the plane. Even though they say that relations between the two countries have improved recently, that book is still considered very subversive, so they were arrested as spies."

"Who put the book there?"

"I think it must have been Hayashi or Nakao. They had had their daughters kidnapped and had no option but to follow the gang's instructions, but I think one of them must have gotten a copy of Mao's book and hidden it in the plane without the gang knowing in the hope that it would be found. I don't know any details yet, but I am very pleased that whoever it was decided to take the risk. It means that not only will we be able to get the whole gang but the money, too."

"But if they have been arrested as spies, will the authorities be willing to return them to us?"

"I don't think you need to worry about that. I will have the Foreign Ministry explain the situation and you can fill them in on any details when you get there."

* * *

It was another week before Totsugawa and six other detectives finally got permission to go to Taiwan and pick up the gang of kidnappers.

The sun at the airport was scorching and he dreaded to think what it must be like when he arrived at the other end. It was only two weeks since the Mystery Train had disappeared, but it felt like much longer.

"Come to think of it, this will be the first time that I actually meet one of the gang," Totsugawa said to Honda, who had come to see him off.

"Yes, now that you mention it, the only contact we have had with them was on the phone."

"Well, I am certainly looking forward to meeting them in person and seeing what they are like."